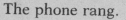

The phone rang.

"Miss Anderson? This is Lieutenant Barringer, Los Angeles Police Department." It was hard to hear him over the T.V. The Lieutenant was saying something about bodies. "How many other patients were staying at the sanatorium?"

"Five." There was no draft, but Dorothy was shivering.

"Can you give me their names, please?"

"Yes." Now she could feel a hint of an air current. Dorothy started to scream . . .

In a moment there were four things open in the apartment. The bathroom window. The door of the closet. The kitchen drawer where the butcher knife was kept. And the jugular vein in Dorothy's throat.

The T.V. in the living room promised that tomorrow would be fair and warmer.

Look for these Tor books by Robert Bloch

THE NIGHT OF THE RIPPER
NIGHT-WORLD

NIGHT-WORLD

ROBERT BLOCH

A TOM DOHERTY ASSOCIATES BOOK

NIGHT-WORLD

Copyright © 1972 by Robert Bloch

First Tor printing: December 1986

A TOR Book

Published by Tom Doherty Associates, Inc.
49 West 24 Street
New York, N.Y. 10010

Cover art by Joe DeVito

ISBN: 0-812-51570-6
CAN. ED.: 0-812-51571-4

Library of Congress Catalog Card Number: 70-189750

Printed in the United States of America

0 9 8 7 6 5 4 3 2 1

This book is for
Zander
who will probably
never read it.

CHAPTER 1

The sun was dying in the west and its blood stained the sky.

I could have been a poet, he thought. *A writer*. But that would have been a waste, a great waste of his talent. A writer's life is short—limited to the life of the paper on which his words are inscribed, and the memory-span of his readers. Paper is brittle and soon crumbles to dust, and the worms eat memories.

Who eats the worms?

Time. Time is the enemy. Time eats the worms, time eats the paper, time eats the sun. Time was eating him, bit by bit, piece by piece, day by day.

Time gnawed at him by night, here in this miserable little room. They called it a room, but of course it was really a cell. A cell with wire-mesh windows through which a dying man could watch the dying sun.

They told him he was here for his own good, and the locked door was a protection against the other patients. But it couldn't protect him against time. Gnawing away, night after night, so that he couldn't sleep. And it couldn't protect him against his protectors. They had a key.

Any hour of the day or night they could come and get him—take what remained after time finished feasting. Draining his blood. For tests, they told him. Did they really expect him to believe that? He recognized them for what they were, these creatures seeking his life's blood for their own existence. They had cast aside their cloaks for robes of white, and they drew their nourishment with needles rather than with pointed teeth, but they were vampires.

Worse than vampires. For they were feeding on his brain too. *ECT*. Electroconvulsive therapy. The scientific term for shock treatment which is the polite euphemism for strapping you down and shooting electricity into your brain to eat away your mind. They took his body and put it in a cell, they took his blood and put it in a test tube—now they wanted to take his brain and put it in a machine.

But they failed. He could still remember the past. And he could still plan for the future. Night after sleepless night here in his room, he planned.

It was perfection, his plan, it was sheer poetry, yet he wouldn't write it down. *Instructions for the Blind—Please Read Carefully.* They must not see his plan, must not suspect. He had it all hidden away in a secret place. The darkest place in the world is the inside of a human skull.

Everything is safe inside your skull. Because it's protected by a mask called a face, and the face responds the way they want it to respond. It smiles at jokes, sobers at the sight of unpleasantness, assumes a properly respectful look in the presence of authority. And the face has a mouth, and the mouth says what the doctor wants it to say. It doesn't even whisper about the plan. *Yes, Doctor, I think I'm much better. I'm beginning to feel like my old self again.*

Nobody wants you to really tell it like it is.

They want you to tell it like they think it *should* be. A model patient: quiet, cooperative, showing distinct signs of improvement. The mouth knows how to make it sound that way.

And by so doing, it helps with the plan. Doctor doesn't know. Nurse doesn't suspect. Orderly hasn't a clue. As long as the face is calm and the mouth says the right words, nobody realizes the truth. That the mouth is just part of a mask, and behind the mask there is a skull and inside the skull is . . .

Inside the skull is everything. Turn it upside down—dump out the contents the way you empty a barracks bag, a woman's purse. What do you find? Something for everyone.

Mysticism. *My horoscope tells me not to believe in astrology.*

Science. *Ornithology is for the birds.*

Literature. *Pornography makes strange bedfellows.*

Philosophy. *Actions speak louder than four-letter words.*

He knew what the doctor would say. He'd said it so often during their sessions. "You're using words as a shield. Obfuscation is a defense mechanism. You talk to avoid saying anything."

What did he expect?

Suppose he told the doctor he'd been thinking about Jimmy Savo. Doctor probably wouldn't even remember the name.

Jimmy Savo. A stage comic of the past. Little man, did pantomimes which reminded critics of Chaplin. Like the one he did in a picture that turned up on the late TV. Jimmy Savo, doing his famous routine to the old song, "River, Stay 'Way From My Door."

You'd have to explain that to the doctor. And then you'd have to explain why Jimmy Savo reminds you of the famous mass murderers of history.

They *are* famous, of course. People who couldn't possibly tell you who was President of France fifty years ago can still recognize the name of Landru. Who remembers that Gilles de Retz rode with Joan of Arc—but who forgets that he was Bluebeard? People are still guessing at the identity of the Cleveland Torso Slayer. And it wasn't too long ago that the papers made a big thing over the theory that Jack the Ripper was really a member of the British nobility.

He was, of course. In a world of victims, the killers are the true aristocracy. That's the one lesson of history: the real hero deals in death. The lion is King of Beasts, not the lamb. And to you, Jimmy Savo sang a different song. "Ripper, Stay 'Way From My Whore."

You can't tell this to the doctor. Not to

him, that dedicated healer, that self-professed lover of humanity! We're all lovers of humanity, of course, each and every one of us. But what most of us forget is that each man kills the thing he loves. The coward does it by dropping a bomb from a plane five miles in the air—the brave man uses a knife, five inches from his prey.

Now hear this, Doctor. And hear this, all you kings, emperors, presidents, admirals, generals, commanders-in-chief. Listen to the words unspoken:

"I shall not kill because you order me to kill; because you issue me a uniform, a weapon and a command. That is fraud.

"I shall not kill because of something that happened between me and my mother, father, sister, brother, wife. That is Freud, and he is a fraud, too.

"I shall kill because I am a brave man. And a brave man is true to his nature.

"It is the nature of man to be free, to resent confinement. It is the nature of man to oppose hypocrisy and injustice. I shall kill in the name of all mankind—all mankind confined hypocritically and unjustly in asylums, prisons, hospitals, rest homes. I shall kill in the name of those who have been punished for their courage in openly defying society. In the name of those who are labeled misfit and unfit. In the name of the bastard buried away in an orphanage and the millions dying neglected and forgotten, institutionalized merely because they have committed the crime of growing old.

"I believe in the principles of democracy. One man, one vote. And mine is a vote of protest—a vote that will register and be remembered. Mass murderers are famous.

"Big talk? But I haven't said a word, not to anyone. Even those who will aid me in my plan do not remotely realize my purpose or the full meaning of the part they will play in executing it."

Executing. That's the word . . .

That was the word.

And now, with the night falling, it would become a deed.

He stared at the dying sun and thought of what else would be dying soon.

Very soon.

CHAPTER 2

After lunch Karen went back to the office.

She blinked her way through the smog-shrouded streets without conscious protest; it was always smoggy in downtown Los Angeles, or almost always. On a clear day you can see your eye doctor.

Karen's office was in a high-rise owned by a savings and loan firm. There seemed to be thousands of such new buildings springing up all over the city in the past few years, and if they were laid end to end it would merely be the expected consequence of another earthquake.

Karen accepted the possibility as she accepted the smog; it really wasn't her worry. And it really wasn't Karen's office she was going to. The name on the door of the tenth-floor suite was Sutherland Advertising Agency, Inc.

She opened the door and moved through the reception room, nodding at Peggy behind the glass partition. Like all such receptionists, Peggy had been chosen for her display value as a beautiful birdbrain. Peasant under glass.

Peggy offered her an official smile of welcome, second class, and pressed the buzzer releasing the lock on the unmarked door at the far right side of the room. Karen turned the knob and entered the corridor beyond.

Now she was in another world. Suther Land, she called it, in the private geography of her mind. The long corridor down which she passed was like a highway in a strange and secret kingdom.

Behind the big oak-paneled double door was the throne room of the ruler, Carter Sutherland III. One of the strange things was that the room didn't contain a desk: in the realms of business, the mark of supremacy is an office without such a demeaning device of drudgery. All a modern ruler needs is a gracious and ostentatious setting for his bar, his intercom and his dictating machine. A dictator—that was Sutherland's true function. Of course rulers seldom spend much time in throne rooms, and one of the secrets was that the biggest office in the Sutherland Advertising Agency, Inc., was usually unoccupied. Karen had seen the man only twice during the four years she'd worked here, and not at all since he'd suffered a stroke on his yacht six months ago. Since then, the agency business had increased almost twenty percent, but that could have been mere coincidence.

Karen moved down the hall past the oak-paneled single doors of the next-largest offices. There were five of these, for the five account executives. Account executives had desks, but in deference to their rank, the desk tops were bare of everything except a telephone. The clutter of paperwork accumulated on the smaller desks of their personal secretaries. And like their superior, the account executives were seldom to be found in the office, although their secretaries could always reach them and intercept calls from their wives.

Farther along the corridor were the domains of the Art Director, the Media Director, the Copy Chief. Linked by a commonly shared meeting room, their quarters were smaller, but very definitely occupied. The individual doors were constantly opening and closing with the comings and goings of printers, engravers, sales reps, messengers and lesser staff personnel carrying memos in and out. Sometimes the meetings—and the profanity—spilled over into the hall, but Karen was used to sidestepping the huddles that threatened to block her progress.

Now she turned the corner into the angled corridor beyond and walked along a row of doorless cubicles lining either side—a series of one-windowed cells barely large enough to contain a filing cabinet, two chairs, and a small desk or drawing board for the individual occupants. Hardly impressive, but then artists and copywriters weren't expected to impress anyone; they merely did the creative work which kept the agency in business.

At the far end of the second corridor, Karen stepped into her own niche, put her purse in the desk drawer, pushed the telephone to one side, and sat down to study the approved and initialed rough layout for a full-page black-and-white scheduled to run in the fashion magazines listed in the accompanying memo and work-data sheet. She glanced at the notes and suggestions, then studied the rough, trying to visualize the finished artwork.

In the foreground, arms folded defiantly across his bare chest, a scowling young man with shaggy hair tumbling across his forehead, the slitted stare of his heavy-lidded eyes suggesting the acid-head. Striped trousers, very tight in the crotch, just suggesting.

Behind him, the girl—all angularity and elbows, hands on hips and legs outthrust. Long straight hair strand-strung on either side of exaggeratedly high cheekbones and sullen slash of mouth. The young witch, suffering from malnutrition or stardom in an Andy Warhol film.

Midway between the two, a chopper or bike. Not a motorcycle—only the pigs ride motorcycles; *we* ride hogs.

Karen made a mental note of the distinction: pigs are bad, hogs are good. If she referred to the machine at all in the copy block, she must remember that. On the other hand, the ad was for the striped pants, and she'd better concentrate on the merchandise. She began to run through phrases, discarding as she went. Dig, bag, with it, doing your thing—last year's vocabulary, but a dead language today. And the Now Generation was presently known as the Beautiful People. Their clothes would be heavy, or funky. Gear. Karen reached for pad and pencil and jotted down a tentative headline—*Geared for Action*.

No sense bothering with an actual description of the trousers; no one buys striped pants, they buy a *look*. And the look was—what? *In deep. Thrust. Put it all together*—and today's lexicon of popular phrases sounded like a description of the activities in a whorehouse.

On the other hand, who was she to pass judgment? *This* was a whorehouse, Karen reminded herself, a whorehouse pandering to the appetites of youth. And what she was doing was whoring. Next year the phrases would change—but she would still be a whore. Unless she got out of here and took up an honest profession, like prostitution. Meanwhile she needed the money, Bruce needed the money, and she'd better write the copy.

The phone rang. Karen uncradled it.

"Sweetheart?"

She recognized the voice, and the approach, of the Copy Chief.

"Yes, Mr. Haskane."

"Girnbach just called. They want to see copy when they look at the rough this afternoon."

"I'm working on it now. Give me another twenty minutes."

"Beautiful! My place or yours?"

"I'll bring it over as soon as I'm finished."

"Don't bother to knock. There'll be cold champagne and a warm mattress waiting."

Karen let the Copy Chief hang up without giving him an answer. Poor Haskane—she understood his hang-up only too well. A pudgy, balding little man, caught in the middle of the generation gap. A potbelly with no stomach for pot.

And it must be doubly hard for Haskane to be working with constant reminders of what he was missing, surrounded by ads for hot pants and never glimpsing or grasping the reality. He'd be jealous of the agency's account execs with their location trips for magazine ad spreads, their expense accounts for a week in Cannes to photograph a nude model holding a light bulb which, like the girl, was AC-DC. Haskane supplied the word, they enjoyed the deed. No wonder he was aggressive on the phone.

Karen wondered what would happen if she ever took him up on one of those verbal passes. The poor bastard would probably drop dead on the way to a motel. Then again, he might surprise her.

Worse still, she might surprise herself. After all, it had been a long time since she'd gone the cold champagne and warm mattress route, and how could she be so sure of her own response? Wasn't she subject to the same pressures as the man she presumed to pity? Selling sex and never buying; always a bridesmaid and never a bride. She'd been a bride once—

Mrs. Karen Raymond. Now she was a wife. A wife in name only, isn't that how they say it?

To hell with them. And to hell with Ed Haskane and his roll in the hay. She was as square as he, probably; not old, not ugly, but just as hung-up in the outmoded mores of her own background.

Karen shook her head and dismissed the subject. Turning to the desk, she fed paper and carbon into the machine. For the next twenty minutes she concentrated on the picture of the scowling, half-naked young man and his unkempt companion, dutifully ignoring the impulse to caption the ad *Me Tarzan—You Ape*.

The electric portable hummed and she murmured, and at last the page was covered with breathless prose celebrating the ineffable glories of a pair of striped pants, complete with crotch-phrases, very tightly written.

Karen ripped the copy out, deposited one carbon in her desk drawer, then clipped the other carbon and the original to the top of the rough layout. She rose and started for the door, and it was then that the phone rang again.

She moved back to her desk, picked up the receiver, listened.

"Mrs. Karen Raymond?"

"Mrs. Raymond speaking," she said.

"One moment, please."

And then the other voice came on, and she listened again and said yes, and yes again, and thank you very much. Her voice didn't tremble.

But when she put the phone down, she almost missed the cradle because her hand was shaking so.

Walking down the hall to Haskane's office was like walking under water, and when she reached down to turn the doorknob, her hand was still shaking.

But she got the door open, got into Haskane's office, got through the meaningless mumble of conversation about the ad.

Haskane's voice was faint and his moon-faced features were wavery and distorted like those of a puffy-faced fish swimming behind the glass of an aquarium. Karen gathered that he liked the copy and would have it retyped for presentation to the client late this afternoon. And would she like to stick around and sit in on the meeting, just in case there were any suggestions for changes?

Karen was drowning, she was going down for the third time, but she came up at the last moment, gasping for breath.

Haskane frowned up at her. "What's the matter?"

"If you don't mind, I'd rather skip the meeting. I want to leave early today."

"Headache?"

"Yes." Karen gulped air.

"Okay. I don't think there'll be any problems. You run along."

"Thanks." Karen flashed him a grateful look, then turned away.

Too bad she couldn't tell the truth.

It was just that she didn't want to see the look on his face if she said, "Sorry, but I've got to run out to Topanga Canyon. I've just had word that my husband may be released from the asylum."

CHAPTER 3

According to the late Edgar Cayce, the area known as Southern California may soon sink beneath the sea.

Ordinarily, Karen dismissed the prophecy as she dismissed the dangers of smog and seismic disaster, but now she wasn't so sure. Whipping along the Hollywood Freeway she wondered if perhaps the prediction hadn't already come true, because she was moving underwater again. On her right, the high hills wavered; on her left, the Capitol tower shimmered; and the road ahead of her was a blacktopped blur.

Only the speed of the car itself reassured her that she was still enveloped by the element of air, and her breathing quickened as she tried to clear her head. Common sense told her to pull over to the shoulder of the freeway, or at least seek the nearest off-ramp, but there wasn't time. Not if Bruce might be released.

If Bruce might be released—

Karen sensed the approaching division in the road ahead and swerved into the right-hand lane which led her into the Ventura Freeway. The midafternoon traffic was just beginning to build up, and she fought to focus her attention on the road. Her vision sharpened, but there was still a blurring of the inner eye, a constant awareness of the inner depths. She felt as if her life was passing in review.

Life? What life was there to remember? There had been a little girl once, a little girl who went to Disneyland with Dad and Mom. But Dad and Mom were in their graves, and the little girl was suddenly a tall, leggy blonde on the UCLA campus, majoring in journalism. Karen tried to visualize the campus, and the waves rose quickly, obscuring it from the mind's eye.

Then Bruce appeared, moving towards her slowly, and they walked hand in hand, moving together slowly under the bursting pressure of the water, little bubbles of laughter rising from their lips until those lips were joined briefly—so very briefly . . . Then she was alone again, working at the agency, and that's when she'd tried to ride out the storm, don't make waves, and—

For God's sake, stop! Karen told herself. *Quit playing with words. You're not writing ad copy now, and you're not drowning in anything except self-pity.*

Karen blinked into accelerated awareness, and moved into the righthand lane leading north on the San Diego Freeway. No more word games now. She knew what she was doing, knew where she was going.

As she eyed the upcoming ramp, a plane snarled overhead, swooping down in a plunging path just above the freeway. Karen lost sight of it as she took the ramp and descended to make a left turn under the freeway on the street below.

Moving at half her former speed, she was suddenly conscious of the hot, acrid air of the San Fernando Valley; she'd come out of her imaginary underwater kingdom into an actual desert. Once, not too long ago, the Valley had been a sandy wasteland. Then a million hardy pioneers invaded it, planting their sickly shrubbery and their crackerbox houses. But all the supermarkets, the bowling alleys, the auto-repair shops, drive-in movies, drive-in hamburger stands, drive-in mortuaries, couldn't disguise the fact that it was still a desert. And the sand still blew across the parking lots of the shopping centers where the sons of the hardy pioneers purchased striped trousers like the ones Karen immortalized in her copy.

Karen drove west against the sun, turned north at the stoplight and proceeded past the expanse of the airport on her right, where the swooping plane now lumbered to a landing. She turned in at the third gate and pulled up near a cluster of small one-engine aircraft grouped around a tin-roofed hangar, inert metal bees before their hollow hive.

Adjoining the hangar was a clapboard rectangular outbuilding, its side displaying paint-flaked lettering—*Raymond's Charter Service.* Above the open doorway was a smaller sign labeled *Office.* Standing in the doorway, squinting into the sun as she watched Karen approach, was Rita Raymond.

Seeing her, Karen told herself for the hundredth time, *she looks like Bruce.* And for the hundredth time she caught herself hesitating momentarily as she drew near. Because she knew that, despite the striking resemblance in features, Rita wasn't like Bruce at all.

The tall, darkhaired woman with the deeply tanned face and somber brown eyes was dressed in boots, levis, and a faded short-sleeved shirt, but the ensemble couldn't disguise the fullness of her hips and the ripe roll of her breasts; the eyes and nose and mouth might be Bruce's, but the body was very much her own. As far as Karen knew, Rita's body was indeed extremely personal property, for she'd never seen Bruce's older sister with an escort. If indeed she had a sex life, it was as well hidden as her sexual attributes were well displayed. Yet she was capable of deep affection—she loved planes, loved the mechanical tinkering she lavished upon them, loved flying, loved her brother—

But not me, Karen told herself. And hesitated again, sensing Rita's level stare.

It took conscious effort to keep moving forward, to force a smile and a greeting.

"So you've heard the news," Rita said.

"Yes." Karen faltered. "They called you too?"

"Doctor Griswold phoned me last night."

"Last night?"

Karen couldn't suppress the surprise in her voice. But Rita's expression was unchanged. She stepped to one side and gestured.

"Come on in."

Karen entered the office, and Rita waved her to a seat next to the big electric floor fan. As Karen sat down, she became acutely conscious of its powerful drone and the blast of air which rattled the flight charts against the side wall. "I suppose you're planning to go up there," she said.

"Of course. I'm on my way."

"Now—tonight?"

"I left work as soon as I got the message." Karen shifted uncomfortably beneath Rita's level stare, and the breeze from the fan ruffled her hair. "Did you think I'd put it off a moment longer than I had to?"

"No." Rita shook her head. "I told Griswold you wouldn't wait."

"But I *have* waited—it's been over six months. Don't you think I'm entitled to see my own husband?"

"It's not a question of being entitled," Rita said. "This is a medical matter."

"Doctor Griswold told me I could come. He *wants* Bruce to see me. Didn't he explain that to you? Bruce's reaction will help determine whether or not he's ready to be released."

"I know." Rita lit a cigarette and inhaled deeply. "I was just thinking about the last time you saw him."

"But Bruce was ill then—we both know that.

And now he's well again. You told me so yourself—"

Rita exhaled, and the fan blew the smoke into a gray halo dissolving to frame her face. "I told you he seemed quite rational when I visited him. And each week he's showed more improvement." The halo dispersed and Karen could see the level stare again. "You've got to remember one thing, though. I'm his sister. He never had any reason to be hostile to me."

"What's that supposed to mean?" Karen felt a tightening in her jaw and temples. "Are you trying to say that I'm responsible for what happened?"

The only reply was the deep drone of the fan. And Karen thought, *she's hiding her hatred behind hints. Seeking out my guilt.*

Karen's temples throbbed and her jaw was so stiff she had difficulty getting the words out. But they came.

"All right. I'm responsible for putting Bruce in the sanatorium. You've gone to see him every week, but they told me not to come, and I obeyed. For six months I've stayed away. Now I have permission to go, and I won't put it off. Because if he is ready to leave, then that's part of my responsibility too—making sure he doesn't stay there a moment longer than necessary."

Rita stubbed out her cigarette. "One thing

more." She glanced up, eyes narrowing. "Suppose he isn't ready? Suppose seeing you sets him off again? Are you willing to accept that responsibility too?"

Now it was Karen's turn for silence, but the echo of the question lingered.

"Why did Griswold call you first instead of me?" Karen said finally.

"Because I've been seeing Bruce all along, and he wanted my opinion before going ahead."

"And you gave it to him, didn't you?" Karen's voice was almost a whisper. "You told him you didn't think Bruce was ready to see me."

"I told him the truth," Rita said. "I told him that in my opinion he'd be taking a big risk in bringing you face to face with Bruce this way, without any advance warning. He said he'd think it over."

"Then when he called me today it meant he'd made up his mind." Karen rose. "If he's willing to take the chance, so am I."

"It's not you and Griswold who'll be taking the chance," Rita said. "It's Bruce. Can't you see that?"

Karen started to move towards the doorway and Rita stood up quickly, intercepting her, strong fingers digging into Karen's arm. "I'm warning you—stay away from my brother—"

Karen jerked her arm free. "He's my husband," she said. "And I want him back."

"No—don't go—"

Rita's harsh voice blurred in the drone of the fan as Karen pushed past her and hurried out. Rita made no move to follow, but when Karen slid behind the wheel of the car, she thought she heard Rita call out to her. The sound of the motor made it impossible to hear Rita's voice, just as the gathering twilight made it impossible to see the expression on Rita's shadowed face.

Karen wheeled the car around against the dying sunset and drove quickly through the exit gateway, turning right at the street beyond. She headed south, into the dusk.

And now the night came quickly.

CHAPTER 4

The moon was rising over the hills when Karen turned off the highway onto the little side road leading into the forest.

In the distance she caught one last glimpse of the lights of the place where she'd stopped for gas and a sandwich. Then the distant glimmer disappeared. Fog swirled over the winding roadway ahead, and Karen cut her high lights, reducing her speed to a cautious crawl as the car ascended around sudden curves.

There was no traffic here, no sign of habitation in the woods below the hilltops. The moon rose higher, and somewhere far off a coyote paid it a mournful tribute.

The fog was quite thick by the time Karen reached the fork, but she recognized the small, inconspicuous white board sign, lettered *Private Road*, and turned her wheels to the graveled surface snaking through tall trees.

Somewhere amidst the trees she lost the moon, and now there was nothing but the dim headlights against gray gravel. A pair of tiny yellow eyes glared up momentarily from the roadside ahead, then quickly disappeared into the woods beyond, leaving Karen alone.

Suddenly she came to the high wire fence at the end of the road. It was quite an imposing fence, curving off as the eye could follow on either side of an equally high gate, but Karen sensed its purpose and was not surprised. What did surprise her was finding the gate wide open, and for a moment Karen wondered, until she remembered that her coming was expected.

She drove through the gateway and onto blacktop that wound through the wooded grounds. Then the trees thinned out and she found the moon again, peering down at the shadowy silhouette of the house ahead.

It was something more than a house, Karen

acknowledged; whoever built it had realized the dream of a mansion set in solitary splendor. Two-story brick, with an imposing facade, and wings on either side. A millionaire's home, in the days when a million dollars was still a lot of money.

Now it was a home of a different sort—a rest home, as the polite euphemism has it—and its occupants, while not millionaires, were still far from impoverished. As Karen knew only too well, it took money to become a patient in Dr. Griswold's private sanatorium. No wonder residence was limited to a half-dozen or so at a time.

Rounding the driveway, Karen pulled up before the front entrance. The house's silhouette was no longer entirely shadowy; she could glimpse lines of light behind drawn drapes covering the windows—lines which cast a reflection of wire mesh.

Karen opened the car door so that its top-light flooded the interior. For a moment she surveyed herself in the rearview mirror. Hair in place. Makeup fresh—she'd attended to that in the washroom of the cafe. But she did look a bit tired, a bit tense. Ever since leaving she'd made a conscious effort to put the conversation with Rita out of her mind, but phrases still echoed. *Suppose he isn't ready?*

Suppose seeing you sets him off again? A big risk. I'm warning you—

Well, it still wasn't too late. She could close the door, turn the car around, head for home. Home? That empty apartment—she'd rattled around in it alone for the past six months, and that was long enough.

Forcing a smile, she got out of the car, walked up to the front door and rang the bell. No one answered.

She pressed the button once more, heard the muffled chime soften into silence. Only a little after nine o'clock—even though she realized the staff was small, surely they couldn't all be in bed for the night.

Karen reached down to rattle the doorknob and discovered it turning in her hand. The door swung open.

Stepping into the high, dimly lighted hall, she caught a quick glimpse of terrazzo floor, paneled walls and closed doors of dark wood set on either side, a high open staircase ahead. At the foot of the stairs, a floor lamp beside a reception desk. And seated behind it, a woman in a white uniform—the night nurse.

For a moment Karen hesitated, awaiting a greeting. But the nurse said nothing, merely stared at her. As Karen moved towards the desk, she saw that it was more than a stare; the woman was positively glaring at her. Karen found herself forcing the smile as she came up before the desk. The light from the lamp was brighter here, reflecting in the bulging eyes.

The bulging eyes—*and the brown cord looped tightly around the woman's neck*—

Karen gasped; involuntarily, her hand swept out to touch the nurse's shoulder. And the stiffly seated figure fell face forward across the desk.

No point in screaming. No point in reaching for the telephone on the desk, not when the cord had been ripped free and used as a strangler's noose.

No point in hesitating, either. The time to get out of here was now, with the door still open. Karen turned, and it was then that she saw the smoke.

It curled out and up from underneath the other door, the closed door at the far side of the reception desk. Karen remembered that door from her one previous visit; behind it was Dr. Griswold's private office.

She moved toward it now, wrenched at the knob, flung the door open wide. For an instant her eyes flickered shut, and then she steeled herself to gaze at what lay beyond the threshold.

With a surge of relief she realized the room was unoccupied—and it was not aflame.

The smoke came from the fireplace in the

far wall: the smoke, and the charred, pungent reek of burning paper heaped upon the glowing embers beneath.

There were scraps of paper wadded and discarded all across the carpet, and a score of empty manila folders; more of the same littered the desk top, and a few odd sheets dangled from the open drawers of the metal file-cabinets in the corner of the room.

Now Karen was conscious of another scent— had something been spilled across the contents of the fireplace to start the blaze? Something that wasn't kerosene or gasoline, something with an acrid stench she couldn't recognize?

Karen advanced, staring down at the blackened bits of paper that remained. There was nothing to indicate the source of the other odor, the source of the buzzing which sounded faintly but persistently in her ears.

The buzzing—

Karen turned and saw the small door opposite the fireplace, saw the flood of light from beneath it. The buzzing came from behind that door.

Almost before she was consciously aware of her movements Karen was at the door, opening it.

A chair was set in the center of the small, white-walled room; a very special chair with padded arms and headrest, a chair with wiring apparatus extending from it like the threads of a spider web.

Karen recognized it for what it was, a unit set up for electro-shock therapy. The buzzing sound emanated from the cabinet behind it, the cabinet from which the wires sprang. Each wire terminated in electrodes, clamped to the bare skin of the temples and neck and wrists of the figure strapped into the chair. Karen recognized the figure, too.

"Doctor Griswold!"

Griswold didn't reply. He merely sat there, the buzzing current throbbing through him, his rigid body pulsing ever so slightly with the force of the discharge. The electrodes were fastened into place by strips of surgical tape, but there were no sponges beneath them to shield the skin. And now, Karen realized the source of the other scent.

It was the odor of burning flesh.

CHAPTER 5

When Karen ran out of the sanatorium her only thought was to get away.

It wasn't even a thought, merely an impulse as blind as the panic which prompted it, as blind as the fog she fought as the car careened along the winding wooded road leading back to the highway.

In a way, the difficulty of driving was a blessing; fighting the wheel somehow helped to fight the panic, and by the time she reached the fork in the road, Karen was almost calm. The dimmed fluorescence of the service station indicated that it was closed for the night, but she saw the outside phone booth and realized she must stop and make the call.

Later Karen couldn't remember exactly what she'd told the police, but it was enough to get action. She wouldn't give them her name, though she did promise to stay there until they arrived.

Of course she had no intention of staying; she'd made up her mind before placing the call. Once the authorities were notified, it was their problem. What had Bruce said about the service—do your duty, stay in line, and never volunteer? Well, she'd done her duty and now it was up to them. She couldn't afford to stay because staying would mean getting involved. And involving Bruce. Not with his record and case history!

So she hung up on them in mid-sentence and walked back over to the car and climbed in, certain that by the time anyone reached the station she'd be too far away to find.

What she didn't anticipate was that she wouldn't be able to start the car.

It wasn't the gas or the carburetor or the engine. The problem was simply that her fingers trembled so she couldn't turn the key in the ignition. Karen sat there quite calmly, completely self-possessed except for the fact that she was shaking uncontrollably. There was no sensation at all, only a numbness. *You're in shock*, she told herself.

If she could sob, if she could scream, then perhaps movement would be possible. But there was only the ceaseless shuddering when she fumbled with the key; the shuddering which evoked images of Griswold's body, throbbing and pulsing. When she glanced up at the rearview mirror she could see his corpse-eyes staring out at her.

Karen closed her own eyes, clenched her hands together in her lap, and shook.

She was still sitting there when the patrol car came flashing out of the fog.

There were three men in the car, and Sergeant Cole was very polite and soft-spoken, waiting patiently until she managed to open her purse and produce her driver's license. She still couldn't control her fingers completely, but oddly enough her voice was firm. At first she flatly refused to accompany them back to the rest home, but Sergeant Cole said he'd have one of his men drive her in her own car, and no, she wouldn't have to look at the bodies.

The officer who drove Karen to the sanatorium was a squat, burly middle-aged man named Montoya. His younger and slimmer companion, Hyams, rode beside her in the back seat.

Karen hadn't expected a double escort, and at first she was a bit confused, until she realized it was a precautionary measure. The thought hit hard, jarring her out of one sort of shock and into another.

She was a suspect.

Karen tensed, shifting uneasily in her seat, waiting for one of her companions to break the silence, to start asking questions.

But there were no questions. Montoya chewed gum and concentrated on the road ahead, following closely behind the patrol car in the fog. Hyams seemed to be relaxing beside her, half-asleep. It was only when she reached into her purse for a handkerchief that his hand dropped instantly to the seat, only inches away from the revolver butt protruding from his holster. Karen caught his eyes and he smiled, but the hand stayed there for the remainder of the drive.

And when at last they parked in the driveway before the big house, Hyams continued to sit beside her.

"Wait here," Cole told him, when he climbed out of the patrol car. He nodded at Montoya. "Let's go."

The front door was ajar—Karen realized for the first time that she hadn't closed it on her way out—and the two men disappeared inside. Karen stared after them, twisting her handkerchief between her fingers. Hyams said nothing, but she was conscious that his eyes were following her movements.

It seemed like a long time before Sergeant Cole came out of the house again. But when he did he was moving quickly, legs scissoring a path to the patrol car. Opening the door, Cole slid across the front seat and a moment later Karen could hear the crackle of the squawk box. She couldn't catch what he was saying, but the message was a lengthy one. She wondered if he'd located any of the other staff members or patients, and if so, what he had learned.

Finally he came around to her car and nodded at Hyams to roll down the window on his side.

"Would you come in now, please?"

The question was addressed to Karen, but it was Hyams who nodded. All very courteous, very correct. And if Karen refused, they would be equally courteous and correct as they dragged her into the house.

Or was she being unfair? It seemed so when they entered the hall, because Sergeant Cole deliberately moved before her to shield her from the sight of the reception desk beyond.

He was, she realized, keeping his promise that she wouldn't have to look at the bodies.

"This way," he said, indicating an open doorway on the left. As Hyams led her toward it, she caught a glimpse of Montoya descending the open staircase at the far end of the hall. It seemed to Karen, even in the dim light, that his swarthy face was unnaturally pale, but perhaps she was imagining that.

Sergeant Cole nodded at Montoya as he approached. "They're on the way now. When they get here, I want them to go ahead, S.O.P., the works. I'll be with them as soon as I can. But unless you run into something we've missed, tell them I'm not to be disturbed."

"Right," said Montoya.

Cole stepped aside, gesturing Karen through the doorway, then followed her with Hyams.

The room beyond was obviously a study, with floor-to-ceiling bookshelves built into two of the walls. Drawn drapes covered the windows of the third wall, and the fourth—at the far end—held a grouping of diplomas and medical certificates in ornate frames. Karen glanced at the desk and the two heavy, old-fashioned leather armchairs before it, realizing she'd seen this setting before. She'd been in this room with Bruce, at the interview preceding his commitment.

But now Sergeant Cole was moving to sit

behind the desk, and it was Hyams who stood beside her, not Bruce. Because Dr. Griswold was dead, and Bruce was—

Where is he? Where is he now? She closed her eyes against a silent scream.

"Are you all right, Mrs. Raymond?" Cole's voice was softly solicitous.

Karen blinked and met his glance.

"Please sit down."

She took her place in the chair nearest the desk, conscious of Hyams' close presence.

And while Cole's smile was casual and relaxed, Karen saw that he now held a ballpoint pen poised over an open note pad on the desk. Every movement was unobtrusive, but these men knew exactly what they were doing; Karen remembered how deftly Hyams' hand had descended to poise behind the holster of his revolver in the car.

S.O.P. Standard Operating Procedure. Interrogation of the witness. Witness or suspect? She'd have to be careful, very careful.

"Now, Mrs. Raymond, we'd like you to tell us what happened—"

The odd part of it was that Karen, as she talked, found herself relaxing. She'd anticipated Cole's asking why Bruce was in the sanatorium, and framed her answer in advance, but she hadn't anticipated there'd be no further questions about his "nervous breakdown." Once Karen realized her explanation was accepted, she had no difficulty continuing.

She told about Griswold's call at the office, and, at Sergeant Cole's request, established the time. She also furnished the approximate time for her visit with Rita—and, when Cole interrupted, furnished him with Rita's address and home telephone number.

So far, so good. But now there was the matter of reporting her conversation with Bruce's sister. Rita's warning about the visit, about Bruce's not being ready for release—these were subjects to be avoided at all cost.

But how?

Rescue came from outside, in the form of loudly wailing sirens. And then, from beyond the door, she heard the clatter of footsteps in the hall and the deep murmur of many voices.

Sergeant Cole frowned and gestured to Hyams. "Tell them to hold it down," he said.

Hyams rose and went to the door. He opened it on bedlam, stepped outside. A moment later, the noise subsided noticeably, and Hyams came back into the room. As he closed the door and moved up to seat himself again, Cole glanced at Karen.

"You were saying—?"

It was easy to pick up her story again at the point where she'd left Rita and driven south, easy to provide Cole with a timetable of her movements to jot down on his note pad. The stop for gas, the sandwich, the drive through the fog, her arrival here at the sanatorium.

"Nine o'clock, you said?"

"Approximately. Maybe a few minutes after."

Muffled footsteps again, this time overhead. Cole glanced quickly towards the ceiling, but said nothing. He nodded at Karen to continue.

Now Karen found herself faltering, not because of any necessity to conceal, but with the painfulness of revelation.

Cole's questions guided her step by step through her drive, bringing her to the front door of the house. What happened after she rang the bell?—how did she discover the door was unlocked?—what was the first thing she noticed when she came in?

His questions led her into the house itself. When did she see the nurse?—what was her reaction when she realized the nurse was dead? —did she consider trying to locate a telephone in another room to call the police?

It was symbiosis, she told herself. He fed her the questions and she fed him the answers. But the questions were increasingly difficult to absorb, and she wondered if her answers were coherent.

Karen told him about the smoke, and he wanted to know what she'd noticed first—was it something she saw or something she smelled?

She mentioned her surprise at the sight of Griswold's office, and Cole carefully drew from her a complete description of the room and its contents.

Then came the worst part: the venture into the other room beyond and the discovery of Griswold's body. Karen couldn't stay in that room for long, not even in memory. The evocation of image and odor made her want to run away, and she rushed through her account so that she could reach the point where she *did* run away.

Cole lifted his pen from the note pad and gestured her flow of words to a halt.

"Excuse me, Mrs. Raymond. You say you turned and ran back through Dr. Griswold's office to the hall?"

"Yes."

"What did you do next?"

"I went to the front door."

"Directly?"

"That's right."

Cole's pen halted its progress across the page. He smiled at Karen. "You were quite upset by this time—is that correct?"

"Upset? I was terrified—"

Cole nodded. "Stop and think for a moment. Perhaps there's something you haven't remembered, something else that happened."

Karen shook her head. "I don't think so."

"Did you go upstairs?" Cole murmured.

"No."

"You say you were in a state of panic, almost shock. Isn't it possible you might have done something without full awareness of your actions at the time?"

Karen frowned. "I ran out of the house," she said.

"You're sure you didn't go upstairs earlier—or at any time before you left?"

"Why should I?"

Just then the door opened, and Montoya entered the study. Karen turned in her chair and saw him standing there as Cole glanced past her.

"Sorry to interrupt you, Sergeant."

Cole nodded. "What is it?"

"They're finished with Griswold and the nurse," Montoya said. "But before they wrap things up, they thought you might want to have another look at the other bodies upstairs."

CHAPTER 6

The lights in the interrogation room were very bright. Karen could see the tiny droplets of perspiration forming at Sergeant Cole's graying temples. She could see every wrinkle in the frowning face of the other officer, Lieutenant Barringer, who had joined them there.

Strange. It's the suspect who's supposed to squirm under questioning, but now she felt quite calm. And they were the ones who were sweating it out.

Not that she blamed them for it, under the circumstances. The nurse strangled at her desk, Griswold dead, and two more bodies found upstairs. She knew who they were, now—an orderly named Thomas and an elderly woman patient. The orderly had been stabbed to death, and the patient apparently died of a heart seizure, but of course they couldn't be certain of that. All they knew was that four people had died; three staff members and one patient.

Five other rooms upstairs showed signs of occupancy, so there had been five other patients in the sanatorium. But they were missing.

They were missing, and all their records, all means of identifying them, had gone up in smoke in Griswold's fireplace.

Five mentally disturbed patients gone. Vanished. Only one—Bruce—known by name. And every reason to believe that one or more of those patients was a mass murderer.

But who were they?

And where could they have gone?

No wonder Lieutenant Barringer frowned when Karen shook her head.

"I'm sorry," she said. "I don't know their names. I never even set eyes on any of them. I told you I didn't visit my husband while he was in the sanatorium."

"Why not?"

"Dr. Griswold thought it best if I stayed away. Bruce seemed so disturbed—"

"Disturbed?"

Barringer picked up the word, but Karen couldn't help that. There was no avoiding the subject, and if she didn't speak up, they'd hear it from Rita.

"Of course. That's why he was under treatment, it was a nervous condition. Ever since he came back from Vietnam—"

"Was he a head?"

"No. He never got into drugs."

"You're sure of that?"

"Certainly. I'm his wife—if there was anything like that going on, I'd know."

"Then in what way was he disturbed?"

"Just nerves—"

"Please, Mrs. Raymond. People don't spend six months in a sanatorium unless there's been some kind of diagnosis. Surely Dr. Griswold told you more than that. What were the symptoms? What did your husband do that prompted you to put him away—"

"I didn't put him away! Bruce was the one who wanted to go!"

Hearing the shrill echo of her own voice, Karen realized she was close to hysterics. If she wanted to help Bruce, she would have to control herself.

Subsiding, she watched Barringer ease himself into a chair across the table from where she sat. He glanced at Cole, then turned to her again.

"Sorry, Mrs. Raymond. I know how you feel."

"Do you?"

"Of course. You've had a shock, you're tired, you don't like all these questions." Barringer sighed softly. "Well, neither do we. The trouble is, we've got to come up with some answers. And right now you're the only one who can help us."

"I've told you the truth."

"I believe you."

"Then what more do you want from me?"

"The rest of the truth. The part you haven't told us yet."

"But that's all there is."

Barringer glanced at Cole again. Cole didn't say anything. He didn't have to say anything, neither of them did. They'd just sit here, waiting until she broke down and gave them what they wanted. Sooner or later they'd get to her, and if they got to her, they'd get to Bruce.

Unless—

"Wait a minute." Karen took a deep breath. The two men looked up quickly.

"I just thought of something."

This time it was Cole who flashed a look at Barringer, a look that said, *see, I told you so, she's ready to crack.* But Barringer, playing the game, the old waiting game he knew so well, didn't react. He leveled his stare at Karen.

"Go on."

"I used to call the sanatorium every week for a report. Usually I talked to Dr. Griswold, but sometimes he wasn't available, and I'd speak to his nurse instead. She was in charge of the day shift. I'm sure if you talked to her she could give you the names of the other patients."

Barringer was leaning forward. "What's her name?"

"Dorothy. Dorothy Anderson."

Sergeant Cole was already scribbling on his note pad.

"Any idea where she lives?"

"I'm not sure." Karen hesitated. "But I think I remember her saying something about moving a few months ago. That's right—she was moving into an apartment in Sherman Oaks."

CHAPTER 7

It is a matter of historical record that William Tecumseh Sherman never set foot in Sherman Oaks. He was much too busy marching through Georgia.

Dorothy Anderson envied him.

From what she remembered reading in school, the march through Georgia wasn't exactly a picnic; it had probably been hot as hell, but it couldn't have been anywhere near the temperature of her one-bedroom apartment on the first floor. And the noise the soldiers endured was surely no worse than she suffered every weekend when those two airline stewardesses held open house for their own private army of volunteers recruited from the Swinging Singles bar down on Magnolia.

Dorothy had never seen any magnolias on Magnolia Boulevard. Come to think of it, she hadn't seen many oaks in Sherman Oaks.

The sole reason she had taken the apartment was convenience. It was two blocks from the Freeway, and less than half an hour from the sanatorium, and she figured that every evening by six-thirty she'd be home free.

Only, a hundred and fifty a month doesn't buy much of a home nowadays. Take tonight for example. In spite of the air-conditioning unit wheezing on the wall, the place was like an oven, if you can imagine an oven furnished in early Sears.

As for freedom, what did it amount to? It meant Dorothy was at liberty to shop at the supermarket, haul her groceries home, unpack them, cook her own meal over the ancient stove and sit down to a frozen food dinner, with yummy natural gravy brought to a simmering delight through the miracle of natural gas. That's what the commercials said, anyway. Just for the hell of it Dorothy wondered what it would be like to enjoy a meal with some unnatural gravy, heated with unnatural gas.

She put the thought away; if she wasn't careful she'd start sounding like those poor dingalings at the san.

Dorothy cleared the table, washed the dishes. That was more than the dingalings had to do, because they really weren't poor. They were rich, or their families were rich; had to be, at the prices old Griswold charged. But in return for the money, they got the red-carpet treatment. Run of the house, run of those lovely grounds behind the san. Sure, there was a fence around the place, but there was a fence around everybody now. And if you don't believe it, just try to go somewhere without an I.D., take a trip outside the country without a passport, or turn right on a one-way street routed left. See how far you can march through Georgia today before some redneck sheriff busts you for vagrancy. For that matter, you don't even have to go anywhere to run smack up against a fence—carefully woven of city, county, state and federal tax blanks, insurance premium statements and notices of payments due from the credit card companies.

The poor dingalings didn't have *that* to worry about; they didn't have to cook and eat frozen dinners, or wash plastic plates afterwards.

So maybe they weren't even dingalings;

maybe they knew something she didn't know. Something about letting it all hang out, and not giving a damn who saw. Maybe *she* was the dingaling, spending her own life looking after them. *You don't have to be crazy to work here, but it helps.*

Dorothy stacked the plastic dishes on the plastic liner of the cupboard, then walked six paces into the living room and fiddled with the plastic knobs on the portable television set.

It wasn't that she wanted to watch a particular program, but the noise would help; at least it would serve as a counter-irritant to the sound of the neighbors' stereo booming through the wall.

She could go out, of course, but where? The local movie house was showing a revival of two classic comedies—one dealing with an angry young man who ran around wearing a gorilla costume, and the other dealing with a placid young man who enjoyed sexual intercourse with a pet pig. Artistic and meaningful as these two critic-acclaimed epics might be, Dorothy knew they would only serve to remind her of her patients.

There was, as an alternative, the Swinging Singles bar patronized by the fly girls upstairs. But it was, Dorothy reminded herself, no place for a woman of thirty-nine (*all right, forty-four!*). She'd been there or to similar spots too many times, and always she ended up with a charmer.

The world—at least the *Entertainment Nitely* world of local taverns—was full of charmers. Witty, well-dressed, suntanned men of thirty-nine (*forty-four?*) with just a touch of gray at the temples and a touch of dye or a toupee on top, all driving secondhand sports cars on which they were behind two payments. They were also behind on their alimony, but you didn't hear about that until after you discovered that the handsome suntan ended just below the collar line of their necks, and the trim waistline vanished once the too-tight trousers were removed.

Charm. Funny how few people seemed to know what the word really meant. A formula, a spell created to cast illusion. Something used by magicians, for deception. Dorothy had learned to beware of charmers, learned the hard way about what was hidden underneath the easy smile and the facile flattery. And not just from one-night stands, either; she'd learned it in her day-to-day duties. Far too many of those who ended up at Griswold's sanatorium were charmers. Glib talkers, specializing in sincerity and sentimentality, quickening to remorse and self-reproach and promises of penitence for every misdeed. And beneath the artfully acquired ability to manipulate others, beneath the carefully calculated con, there was the little boy who never grew up, because he never *had* to grow up; who had Mommy and Daddy to tell him how cute he was and to take care of the messes for him. Then, later on, there was always some Dorothy or her equivalent; some dumb klutz ready to listen, to pay up the installments, put up with the lies and the delusions of grandeur. Until, of course, the little boy ran into a problem which charm wouldn't solve. Then he fell apart and ended up, kicking and screaming, locked in a closet—or a prison cell. Or, if somebody could afford it, Dr. Griswold's sanatorium.

Dorothy didn't want any more charmers because she could always see the little boy underneath—the little boy who was incapable of really loving anything or anyone but himself, and who foiled frustration by cutting up cats with a butcher knife.

So she turned on the television and watched professional charmers enact a charade about an ever-so-clever and sophisticated private detective whose skills as a scientific criminologist were deftly demonstrated when he smashed the villain in the jaw and dropped him with a karate cut.

Two more equally superficial shows, and the late news came on. *That* wasn't quite as charming, so Dorothy turned it down. Down, but not off. She still wanted to hear the sound of voices, wanted audible reassurance that she wasn't entirely alone. At thirty-nine—or forty-four—nobody really wants to be alone, come midnight.

Dorothy went into the bedroom and removed the bedspread. She got her nightie out of the closet and hung it in the bathroom. From this point on, her movements were entirely automatic, conditioned by long habit.

The newscaster said something she didn't quite catch about the situation in Asia as she undressed. The account of the demonstration and riot in Washington was muffled by the sound of the spray when she showered. Drying herself with a towel, and slipping on her nightie, Dorothy glanced out through the bathroom doorway; on the television screen an incredibly ugly middle-aged couple were mugging in feigned delight over a jar of instant coffee.

It was almost time for the weather report which would help determine what clothing she'd lay out for the morning. She opened the window in the steamy bathroom and went into the living room so as not to miss it.

The commentator was saying something about a late bulletin. "Patients escaped tonight from a private rest home in Topanga Canyon, leaving four dead."

Dorothy gasped and hastily turned up the volume.

"—victims of what was apparently a suprise murder attack have been identified as Dr. Leonard Griswold, 51, owner and operator of the sanatorium, Mrs. Myrtle Freeling and Herbert Thomas, members of the staff—"

"Oh, my God!" said Dorothy.

Then the phone rang.

She ran into the bedroom and picked up the receiver.

"Miss Anderson? This is Lieutenant Barringer, Los Angeles Police Department."

It was hard to hear over the television set. The Lieutenant was saying something about discovering the bodies.

"I know," Dorothy told him. "I was just listening to it on the news."

The breeze from the bathroom window couldn't reach her but Dorothy was cold all over—cold and trembling. She missed the Lieutenant's next few words and strained to hear.

"—apparently one of the patients, and we need your help in identifying her. An elderly woman, about sixty-five, short, quite thin, wearing rimless glasses—"

"Mrs. Polacheck," said Dorothy. "Frances Polacheck. P-O-L-A-C-H-E-C-K. No, I don't. She was a widow. I think she lived in Huntington Park, she has a sister there."

"How many other patients were staying at the sanatorium?"

"Five." There was no draft, but Dorothy was shivering. "For God's sake, tell me what happened—"

"Can you give me their names, please?"

"Yes." Dorothy took a deep breath. She could feel a hint of an air current. She turned and saw that the door of the bedroom closet behind her was opening.

Dorothy started to scream, but it was too late.

In a moment there were four things open in the apartment. The bathroom window. The door of the closet. The kitchen drawer where the butcher knife was kept. And the jugular vein in Dorothy's throat.

On the television set in the living room, the announcer promised her that tomorrow would be fair and warmer.

CHAPTER 8

The morning sunlight streamed through the window behind Dr. Vicente, haloing his bald head.

Karen, seated across the desk from him, blinked in the brightness. Her sleep-starved eyes were gritty, and she leaned back to avoid the glare. But there was no way of avoiding the direct gaze of the police psychiatrist. Or his direct questions.

"Why was your husband in the sanatorium?"

"Please." Karen shook her head. "I explained everything to Lieutenant Barringer last night. Couldn't you get all this from his notes?"

"I have a transcript of your statement here." Dr. Vicente glanced briefly at the typed sheets on the desk before him. "But it would help if you could give us a little more information." He smiled at her. "For example, you mentioned your husband's nervous condition. That's not very specific. Could you describe his behavior?"

Karen shifted her chair to the left, trying to get the sun out of her eyes. "There's not much to describe, really. It's only that he seemed very quiet. Too quiet."

"Withdrawn?"

"I suppose you might call it that. He spent a lot of time just sitting around. Not reading or watching television—just sitting. He didn't seem interested in seeing our friends, or even going out to dinner or a show. And he got into this habit of sleeping until noon."

"Did he complain of fatigue?"

"No. Bruce never complained. He never talked about how he felt."

"What *did* he talk about?"

"Well—at first he said he was going to send out some resumés, try to set up interviews with people in the industry. He'd been in computer-data work before he went into service. But I don't think he ever actually followed through."

"You never questioned him about it?"

"No. Because I could see there was something wrong, even though he refused to say what was bothering him."

"But you must have discussed it, before you decided to put him in the sanatorium."

Karen forced herself to meet Dr. Vicente's gaze. "Bruce was the only one who decided, really. He knew he had a problem, and he wanted help."

"I see." Dr. Vicente leaned back. "But from what I understand, the sanatorium was rather expensive. Surely you realized therapy was available without charge through the Veterans Administration."

"No—he hated the thought of a veterans' hospital—"

"Why?"

"He said the mental wards were like a prison, only worse. He couldn't stand the thought of being penned in like some animal—"

Dr. Vicente spoke softly. "Had your husband ever been in the mental ward of a veterans' hospital, Mrs. Raymond?"

The grittiness disappeared from Karen's eyes, inundated by sudden tears. "Don't talk about

Bruce that way! I told you he committed himself voluntarily, and Dr. Griswold said he was ready for release. He isn't crazy—he never was!"

It wasn't until she thought about it later than Karen realized Lieutenant Barringer must have been monitoring the interview from another room. But now, as he came through the doorway, all she could see was a tired man who badly needed a shave.

"Not interrupting, am I?" he said.

Dr. Vicente shook his head. Karen blotted her eyes with a handkerchief from her purse.

Barringer moved toward the desk. "Just wanted you to know we're broadcasting the appeal. All radio and television newscasts will carry it throughout the day. We're asking the families of the missing sanatorium patients to get in touch—identify their relatives and give any information they have concerning their whereabouts."

Dr. Vicente sighed. "If I were you, I wouldn't count on them for help."

"Why not?"

"I'm afraid those families probably feel the way Mrs. Raymond does—they don't want to run the risk of possibly incriminating a husband, a wife, a son or daughter. You've got to remember those patients were placed in the sanatorium for the express purpose of keeping their condition a private matter. These murders will only intensify the families' desire to protect their loved ones from possible accusation."

"I realize it's only an outside chance," Barringer said. He glanced at Karen. "That's why I was hoping Mrs. Raymond here would listen to reason."

Karen glanced up quickly. "You're the ones who aren't reasonable. Just because Bruce was a patient at the sanatorium—that doesn't mean he was involved in those murders. Why should he kill those people and run away when he was ready to be discharged?"

"You're jumping to conclusions—"

"What about you?" Karen faced Barringer directly. "This morning you said Dorothy Anderson was killed to keep her from talking. Where's your proof? People are murdered every day—maybe it was just coincidence."

Lieutenant Barringer shrugged. "Griswold's car was missing from the sanatorium last night. We located it about an hour ago—parked on a side street about a block away from Dorothy Anderson's apartment."

Karen turned away, but Barringer's voice pursued her. "Still sound like coincidence, Mrs. Raymond?"

"I tell you Bruce wouldn't harm anyone—"

"We haven't accused your husband." Dr. Vicente rose and moved around the desk to where Karen sat. "All we're saying, all we know at the moment, is that he is one of five escapees from that sanatorium. And that on the basis of evidence presently known, it would appear that one or more of those escapees committed the murders."

"But you admit you don't know which one it is," Karen said.

"That's right." Vicente pursed his lips. "But every indication seems to point to *what* he is. A sociopathic personality. Someone who may appear to behave quite rationally, who may even act with brilliant intelligence most of the time—but becomes utterly ruthless when triggered into violence.

"Make no mistake about it, whoever killed those people knows exactly what he's doing, and why. He's out to destroy all evidence of his identity—anything, and anyone. And that means you yourself are in jeopardy."

"But that's ridiculous—"

"Is it?" Lieutenant Barringer broke in with a frown. "The morning paper carried a front-page story on the slayings. Your name is in it."

Karen didn't say anything, but her hands tightened on the rim of her purse.

"Please don't misunderstand. We're not trying to alarm you. But perhaps now you can realize the importance of cooperation on every level. Your own safety is involved. Anything that you can tell us that might lead to the apprehension of the slayer—"

Karen's fingers pressed into the folds of the purse, but she shook her head. "I've already told you everything I know."

"All right," said Lieutenant Barringer. "I guess we go downtown."

"Downtown?"

Barringer nodded. "I'm going to have to hold you in protective custody."

"No—" Karen rose quickly.

"Sorry. You're a material witness."

"But you already have my statement."

"If there are any further developments in the case, we may have to talk to you again."

"You don't need to lock me up for that! I'm not going to leave town. I've got a job here, you can reach me any hour of the day or night—"

"And so can the person who committed the murders." Lieutenant Barringer shook his head. "It's our responsibility to see that you're not in danger."

"But this could go on for weeks! I'll lose my job—"

"And save your life."

"Please! There must be some other way." Karen spoke hastily. "Suppose you gave me a bodyguard—"

"Have you any idea of the number of men already involved in this case? We're short-handed as it is. What you're asking involves assigning at least three men to you, working on eight-hour shifts. And it's not just man-power, it's the taxpayers' money we have to think about."

"I'm a taxpayer. It's my money, too. And if I lose my position at the agency because of this—" Karen felt the tears, fought them. "Please, you've got to give me a chance!"

Barringer glanced at Dr. Vicente.

"All right," he said. "But I want it clearly understood. No statements to the press, no television interviews. Whoever's assigned to duty with you, you're to follow his orders."

"I promise."

"Better think it over. It's not going to be easy. You won't have any privacy—there'll be someone watching you night and day. And if anything happens—"

"Nothing's going to happen," said Karen, quickly. "You'll see."

She stared at the two men as she spoke,

trying to read their faces, wondering if they believed her.

Not that it mattered.

Because she didn't believe herself.

CHAPTER 9

The weather forecaster had kept his promise.
It was fair and warmer in Los Angeles.

Not that people were thinking about the
weather. They were too busy reading the headline story in the *Times* and listening to the
early newscasts. And, warm as it was, a col-
lective shudder swept across the city. Memories began to stir.

There had been a strangler in Boston, cold-
blooded murderers on the prairie, a rampag-

ing rifleman on a tower in Texas, a psychotic slayer in Phoenix, a killer of migrant workers who filled more than two dozen shallow graves dotting the California farmlands. Somewhere around the Bay Area a slayboy turned homicides into an ego-trip, as he boasted of his tally of victims in letters to the newspapers which he signed with the *nom de doom* of Zodiac. And right here in fair and warmer Los Angeles, people were remembering the Manson family.

All men are brothers—but which brother is named Cain?

An unfair question, perhaps, and an unfair comparison. For Cain slew Abel for personal reasons, unacceptable but understandable.

There was nothing personal about these killings. Cain had become a mass murderer, striking savagely and at random.

In Biblical times, God put a mark upon Cain but did not kill him, and Cain went to dwell in the land of Nod.

Today, God's surrogate, the psychotherapist, puts his mark upon Cain, branding him sociopath, psychopath, multiple schizophrenic, cycloid personality—and Cain is sent to dwell in the asylum.

And now, today, five potential murderers were at large. And their bloody trail led from the distant canyon into the heart of the city itself. The heart began to pulse and pound at the realization of its own vulnerability.

Telephones rang and women exchanged shrill queries. *Did you read the paper, did you hear the news on television, do you think they'll find out who they are, do you think they'll catch them?* Appointments were canceled at the hairdressers' and shopping plans hastily abandoned. *That poor Dorothy Anderson. Remember all those nurses in Chicago? I'm not leaving the house today.*

It was the men who left the house, who did the shopping. Before they went to work, they stopped by the hardware stores and bought locks, install-it-yourself alarms.

And as the day grew warmer, children whined behind closed doors. *Why can't I go outside, Mommy? I want to play. You promised I could go in the pool, remember?*

Mommy shut them up. Shut them up inside, behind closed doors, barricaded from all callers, even the mailman.

The noonday sun was high in the heavens, but Los Angeles stayed at home, listening to the latest news—which was no news at all.

At police headquarters in the West Valley, in Van Nuys, Hollywood, downtown, the reports were coming in from the lab boys. Again, no news at all.

The murderer had been careful about prints. He had worn gloves. The Anderson apartment and the Griswold automobile had yielded no clues, and nothing had been turned up at the sanatorium, though a team was still working. But so far there weren't any leads—and no one had phoned in to volunteer any information.

"Just the usual crank calls," Lieutenant Barringer told Dr. Vicente. He took the last gulp of his coffee and frowned down at the cup. "Why do they always call, Doc? Why is it that every nut in town gets on the phone at a time like this—fake confessions, phoney reports of guys hiding under the bed, old *yentas* telling about their dreams?"

"You touch a nerve, you get a response," Vicente said. "The reaction to violence is usually a violent one, but it takes a variety of forms. People tend to dramatize their guilt feelings, fantasize their fears."

"Save the lecture for UCLA," Barringer said. He shook his head, yawned heavily. "I'm going to get some sleep."

Dr. Vicente hesitated. "There's something I wanted to tell you before you check out."

"Go ahead."

"I contacted Sawtelle this morning. The VA Center has a file on Bruce Raymond."

"Was he a patient?"

"No, not there. But it's a medical discharge, and he was definitely under psychiatric observation before he was released from service. That's all they told me over the phone, but they're getting a transcript to us this afternoon."

"Good."

"Is it?" Dr. Vicente's eyes were thoughtful. "I have no way of knowing what that transcript will show, but one thing is already clear. Whatever was wrong with Bruce Raymond, he obviously didn't make a permanent recovery. That's why he went to the sanatorium."

"You're not telling me anything new," Barringer said.

Dr. Vicente's gaze narrowed. "But, knowing this, you still allowed Mrs. Raymond to go home."

"With around-the-clock surveillance."

"Her husband could be dangerous."

"We're already set up to monitor any calls on her apartment phone. If he tries to contact her directly, there'll be a good man waiting for him."

"You're hoping he does show up, aren't you? That's why you let her go—to use her as bait."

"No comment."

"I'll comment on it. I think it's one hell of a risk."

"She asked for it, remember? And we're giving her every possible protection."

"If you really wanted to protect her, you'd see to it that she was held here."

"Get off my back, Doc." Barringer stood up. "Sure, she'd be better off under maximum security conditions. But that's just part of the job. There's three million other people out there whose phones aren't bugged, who have nobody assigned to stand guard duty, who have no security at all. They've got to be protected, too—and none of them are safe until we nail whoever's reponsible for these killings."

Dr. Vicente shrugged. "You talk as though you were the only man on the case. Between the LAPD and the Sheriff's Department, how many men are working with us? There must be hundreds—"

"And not a single goddam lead for any one of them to go with." Barringer shook his head. "I agree with you, letting that girl go is a hell of a risk. But if it can give us a line on Bruce Raymond or any of the other suspects, it's a risk we've got to take."

"All right." Dr. Vicente moved with Barringer towards the door. "Get some rest."

"I'll do that," said Barringer.

And he did.

*   *   *

Karen sat in the air-conditioned hum of her apartment, staring alternately at the telephone and at Tom Doyle.

The telephone was black and squat and silent.

Tom Doyle was white and tall and silent.

The telephone sat on an end table. Tom Doyle sat on the sofa, but in the past hour he'd come to seem as much of a fixture in the apartment as the phone—just another permanent installation.

Well, she'd asked for it, Karen told herself. There was no reason to resent him or his presence. But she hadn't realized somebody would be breathing down her neck quite so closely. *He's here to protect you, that's his job. Be reasonable.*

Easier said than done. Doyle was reading a magazine, and Karen gave him a sidelong glance of appraisal. Long and lanky, with sandy hair and a pale, freckled face. Probably in his middle thirties. Gray suit, summer weight, with medium-wide lapels. Gray-and-white striped shirt, pale blue tie. Conservative. He didn't look like a detective.

Karen caught herself and frowned. *What's a detective supposed to look like?* She'd watched too much television, she told herself. All those shows with the older, craggy-featured ex-leading man playing the brains and the young, grinning ex-filling station attendant playing the muscles. Racing around in sports cars, up and down the hills of San Francisco, while rock music blasted from the soundtrack.

Doyle didn't drive a sports car, and there was no rock music here—just the humming of the air-conditioner. But he was a detective; the minute they'd arrived he'd examined the front door to see if anyone had forced the lock. Then he checked out the entire apartment, revolver in hand, making sure she stood well to one side as he opened and closed closets, examined the windows. The window in the bathroom was partway raised, and if she hadn't told him at once that she'd left it open before going to work yesterday morning, he probably would have called Barringer right then and there and arranged to drag her back to the station. He was a detective, no doubt about it.

Karen stirred in her chair, her left foot tapping against its base like a nervous metronome.

Doyle looked up. "You don't have to keep me company, Mrs. Raymond. If you want to lie down for a while—"

"I couldn't sleep." Avoiding his eyes, Karen concentrated on the telephone. *Bruce, I know you're out there somewhere. For God's sake, why don't you call?*

Doyle's voice was soft. "Don't worry, I won't

90

touch the phone. If it rings while you're asleep, I'll wake you up and let you answer it."

He was a detective, all right. Or was it just that her reactions were so obvious?

Karen rose, forcing a smile. "Thanks. Maybe I will stretch out for a few minutes." She started toward the bathroom doorway.

"Mrs. Raymond."

"Yes?"

"Better not close your door."

Karen went on into the bedroom. *Don't close your door. Great. And suppose she wanted to go to the bathroom?*

She did just that, moving through the bedroom and leaving the bathroom door ajar. At least he couldn't see her from the living room, not unless he followed her. This was worse than being in jail. Now she could understand how Bruce must have felt in the sanatorium, under observation, someone watching all the time. *Bruce, where are you? I know you've been here.*

She knew because she had lied about the bathroom window. When she had left for work yesterday, it had been closed and locked.

She moved to it now, quietly and cautiously, ears attuned for any telltale sound that would show that Doyle might have gotten up. Carefully, very slowly and deliberately, she eased the window down, exposing the lock, with its telltale bright metal streakings, shining in parallel grooves against the marred, painted surface. The lock had been forced open from outside.

Karen had been sure Bruce had been home the moment she'd seen the partly-open window; she never left the apartment without making certain everything was closed. And if she hadn't had the presence of mind to tell Doyle she'd opened the window, if she hadn't been quick enough to forestall him, he would have done what she was doing now and had confirmation.

Karen took a deep breath. *Confirmation of what? That Bruce had been here?*

It was her first thought at the time. That's why she'd lied to Doyle.

But now, gazing at the forced lock, she had to admit to herself that she wasn't sure. After all, Bruce did have his own key to the apartment. Unless, of course, it wasn't in his possession when he left the sanatorium. Griswold might have placed all of Bruce's personal effects somewhere for safekeeping, and he might not have had the opportunity to locate his key. Even so, would he have risked entering this way?

The murderer of Dorothy Anderson came in through the bathroom window—

Maybe it wasn't Bruce who had forced this lock. Suppose it was the killer?

Karen turned, started back towards the bedroom. She'd better tell Doyle.

Or should she? Her pace slackened and she halted before the bathroom mirror.

She couldn't tell Doyle; it would be an admission of a deliberate lie, and the moment he knew he'd yank her back down to headquarters—to sit there, behind bars, not knowing what was happening, without a chance of hearing from Bruce, without a chance of his ever getting to her.

But what if he did get to her?

What if it *had* been Bruce after all, trying to get to her—trying to get to her and kill her?

Bruce wouldn't do that.

Or would he?

Karen met her own wide-eyed stare in the mirror.

Would he?

That was the real question, the question she'd tried to avoid all along. But she had to face it now, just as she had to face herself in the shimmering glass.

Knowing what had happened, knowing what she did about Bruce—did she think he was guilty?

Slowly, Karen retraced her steps to the window and opened it to its former position. That settled that; Doyle wouldn't realize what had happened. But it still didn't answer the question.

Was Bruce guilty?

She didn't know.

And now, staring through the open window at the empty alleyway, she was afraid to find out.

CHAPTER 10

No news is good news—but not to a reporter.
LAPD had no official statement to issue that afternoon, and neither did the Sheriff's Department. Lieutenant Barringer was unavailable for comment—holed up somewhere for his badly-needed sleep—and Captain Runsvick, fronting for the homicide division, had nothing to offer but advice.

"Play it down," he said. "Sure, we're getting a lot of calls and we'll be checking them out. As soon as we've got something, we'll give it to you. But until we do, no sense spreading rumors."

A few blocks away, the press was faring no better at the Sutherland Agency. Ed Haskane was perfectly willing to talk, but he had nothing to say. Yes, he was Karen's boss, but he'd never met her husband. No, she had never spoken about him except when he was discharged from service; then she'd been very excited that he was coming home. Afterwards, he'd just taken it for granted that everything was fine. He had been shocked to learn that Bruce Raymond was in a sanatorium. What was Mrs. Raymond like? A very bright girl, wrote good copy. All of which might well be true, but it didn't make good copy.

In midafternoon, Tom Doyle closed the door on would-be interviewers at Karen's apartment. They had to make do with neighbors, but no one could tell them very much. Only a few of the women around the courtyard pool could remember seeing Bruce Raymond at all, and nobody had actually spoken to him during his brief stay over six months ago. Apparently Karen was looked upon as a loner; she had no friends here and never came down to the pool herself. When Bruce ceased to put in an appearance, most of the other tenants hadn't even noticed his absence. The few who did merely assumed there'd been a separation or a divorce.

Late in the afternoon a mobile TV unit descended on Griswold's sanatorium. They'd come out in the morning, only to find the place was off-limits, and the situation now was still unchanged. Squad cars guarded the gates, and Sergeant Cole was supervising an investigatory team inside. If anything had been turned up, it wasn't ready for release. The camera crew had already picked up exterior footage during their first run, and there wasn't much point in taking more. They did get a few shots of long-haired local residents clustered across the road, but since the observations of these curiosity seekers were largely confined to mumbled asides about pigs, fuzz and other four-letter commentaries, the visit proved to be a waste of time and film.

It was already dusk when the mobile unit broke its return run downtown to stop at *Raymond's Charter Service*. Once again they drew a blank; patrol cars stood before the entrance, and a uniformed officer politely refused admission to the newscasters. There was some debate inside the mobile unit about the advisability of sticking around until the police left, but it was getting late and the ten o'clock news waits for no man; they'd never be able to put coverage on the air in time.

Inside the office, Rita Raymond happened to glance through the window just as the mobile unit drove away. She didn't say anything about it; she was doing her best to say as little as possible.

But it wasn't easy, not with Sergeant Galpert asking the questions. She didn't care for the sergeant; he had the persistent manner of a terrier worrying a bone.

"You're positive that your brother made no attempt to get in touch with you?"

"He may have tried. All I know is he didn't succeed."

Galpert frowned. "Meaning he might have come here?"

"I haven't seen him." Rita lit a cigarette as she glanced out of the window again. "And neither have your men, apparently." Rita exhaled, and the fan behind her whirred, weaving the smoke into a weblike tracery. "Tell me, Sergeant, isn't it customary to bring a search warrant when you conduct an operation like this?"

Galpert looked as though he was going to growl at her for trying to take away his bone. "You admitted us to the property on your own volition. Of course, if you want to bring up technicalities—"

"I don't want to bring up anything." Rita checked herself; any show of antagonism would only provoke barking and snapping. "Believe me, I'm as anxious to locate Bruce as you are. But I've told you—he hasn't contacted me."

"When was the last time you saw your brother?"

"He's been in the sanatorium since last winter—you know that."

Galpert nodded quickly. "And you visited him there."

"Who told you that?"

"Your sister-in-law."

Rita repressed her frown. Of course Karen would have mentioned the visits, she should have anticipated he'd know about them. No way of holding out now.

"When was the last time you saw your brother?" Galpert repeated.

"Thursday, in the afternoon. I never went on weekends, that's when we get busy here—"

"Last Thursday afternoon." Galpert leaned forward; the terrier had a good grip on his bone now and he wasn't letting go of it. "What happened?"

"Nothing." Rita stubbed her cigarette. "It was a nice day. We took a walk outside, on the grounds."

"Just the two of you? No attendant?"

"It wasn't necessary. He'd been perfectly fine for months—"

"And before that?"

Rita hesitated. "We'd visit indoors, in his room." She shook her head. "Look, if you're trying to get me to say he'd been disturbed—"

"Had he?"

"Of course he had, at first. That's why he was out there to begin with. But he was never violent or irrational like some of the others, not even at the beginning."

Galpert wasn't satisfied with the bone; he wanted the marrow, too. "The other patients—you saw them?"

"No, never. Dr. Griswold had a thing about respecting a patient's right to privacy."

"Then how do you know the others were violent and irrational?"

"Bruce told me. Not all of them, but a few."

"Who, for example?"

Rita's forehead wrinkled. "I'm trying to remember if he ever mentioned anyone by name."

"Think."

"Well, there was one he talked about, several months ago. He'd just come in to dry out."

"Alcoholic?"

"Yes. The reason Bruce mentioned him was

because of the way he ran his business. He was in real estate."

"Here in town?"

"Somewhere in Los Angeles. Culver City, that area."

"What's his name?"

"He did tell me, but I can't recall—"

"What did he say about him?"

"That he had figured out a new way of picking up property cheap. But you don't want to hear about the real estate business—"

"Go on."

"Well, suppose you had a house to sell, and you went to him and told him what you wanted for the property. He'd promise you action if you would give him an exclusive listing—and action is what you'd get. In a day or so he'd bring a couple over, nice middle-aged people with a new car, obviously respectable and responsible. They'd go through your house, and the woman would tell you how much she liked it—just the location they'd been looking for, too. But the man would complain. If you didn't have a pool, he wanted a house with a pool. If you had a pool, he didn't want one. The garage wouldn't be big enough, or he needed copper-pipe plumbing, something like that. And by the time he got through all his objections, he'd offer you a price way below what you were asking—a ridiculous figure.

"So you'd say no, and they'd go away, but the real estate man would tell you not to worry, there were plenty of other prospects.

"Sure enough, in a few days he'd bring over another couple. They'd be driving an older model car and would look a little on the seedy side, but neither of them would complain. And the man would tell you this was just the kind of a house they wanted, only there was a little problem about financing—he'd lost his job in the aerospace industry and in order to swing the deal, you'd have to give him a second mortgage at low interest.

"When they left, the real estate man would reassure you again, tell you to be patient. And after a week or so he'd show up with another couple. Chicano, or maybe black, with several small children. And this would put you off— not because of the ethnic thing, but because it would turn out that they weren't really interested in buying, just in renting on a month-to-month basis.

"Well, by this time you'd be getting a little discouraged, and the real estate man would give you another hard-sell pitch. He'd admit that maybe the market was a little soft right now, things were pretty tough, but houses were being sold and he knew he could scare up a buyer—maybe if you'd shave the price down to a more realistic figure. Perhaps you'd give him an argument on that, but after all he still had a ninety-day exclusive listing, and half of that time had gone by, so you'd have to hold still and wait for him to dig up more prospects.

"Then he'd let you sweat for a few more weeks. If you called him, he'd tell you to cool it, he was doing the best he could. And finally he'd show up again with another couple. A young couple, driving a microbus, long hair, the whole bit. And they'd tell you your pad was beautiful, man, only they didn't have the bread, and how's about a deal where they moved in and looked after the place until you found a buyer?

"After they got lost, you'd sit and wait. And wait. And wait. And when you called the real estate office, your man would always be out and he wouldn't return your call. Until one day he'd come rolling up with a sharp-looking executive type and his wife and they'd go through the house. Just go through it, no comments. Finally the man would ask the price and you'd tell him, maybe even coming down a few thou on it. He wouldn't say a word—just look at his wife. And then they'd turn and walk out.

"After that, you'd wait again. Maybe another month would go by and not even a word. Until finally you'd get a phone call from the husband of the first couple who looked at the house, the nice couple with the new car. He and his wife had been thinking about your place, and if it was still for sale he was still ready to offer you the price he'd quoted—cash on the line.

"Chances are, if you really needed to sell your house, that this time you'd say yes. And sure enough, the real estate man would bring them over again, the papers would be drawn up, the deal would go through escrow, and your house would be sold at that ridiculously low figure.

"What you'd never know is that you'd sold your house to this real estate man. Because the nice couple were his employees. And the others—the seedy couple, the black couple, the young kids, the executive type—were actors."

"Actors?"

"That's right. Professional actors, hired on a per diem basis, to play the roles of prospects. The whole thing was an act he used to buy up properties at a fraction of the market price—so he could resell them on his own at a nice fat profit." Rita shook her head. "How about that? No wonder he got rich."

"Who?"

"Lynch."

Galpert glanced at her quickly. "That's his name—you're sure?"

Rita shook her head. "No, not Lynch. It's—Lorch. His name is Jack Lorch."

Galpert smiled at her. Then he took his bone and went out.

Rita stood in the doorway and watched him drive away. After a moment she turned and went back into the office.

Very quietly, very cautiously, Bruce Raymond emerged from his hiding-place in the cockpit of a plane tied down outside the hangar.

Then he started off into the night.

CHAPTER 11

Jack Lorch walked down the street. Walked slowly, because his feet hurt and because it wasn't safe to run.

It seemed as if he'd been walking forever. Hard to realize that less than twenty-four hours had passed since—

But he didn't want to think about *that*.

He didn't want to think about leaving the sanatorium, or the ride into town in Griswold's car, or about what happened after that car parked on the darkened dead-end street in Sherman Oaks.

Dead end. He didn't want to think about *that*, either.

The important thing was to remember he'd gotten away—running at first, then slowing his pace once he realized he was free.

Free?

Lorch grimaced. What freedom is there for a fugitive from justice? A fugitive from injustice, really. The whole damned police force was looking for him now. In their eyes—those ice-cold official eyes—he was an escaped lunatic and a murder suspect.

Lorch halted under a streetlamp on Washington Boulevard and stared into the plate-glass window of a hardware store. He examined his reflection carefully, wondering what the police would see if they spotted him.

Middle-aged man in a dark blue doubleknit suit. Good enough, because it hadn't wrinkled too badly when he slept hidden under the bushes on the slope of the freeway last night.

His face was puffy and swollen, and he needed a shave, but that in itself was no crime—not yet. Plenty of middle-aged men walking around in need of a shave. And the suit looked respectable, even though he wasn't wearing a tie.

The trouble was, if anyone stopped him, he

had no identification. "Let me see your driver's license." That was always the first thing they said. And when you couldn't come up with one, there was no way. What could you tell the judge? *Your Honor, I plead not guilty on the grounds that I'm a pedestrian.*

All right, so he was overdramatizing. They'd settle for credit cards, your Social Security number. But he had no cards with him at all. Not that his credit wasn't good; hell, he still owned the company, the money was still rolling in, even at the sanatorium he got regular reports from his accountant. Blix was a smart operator, he kept his eye on the business.

But Blix was probably a little too smart. If Lorch had given way to his first impulse and gone to Blix for help, the bastard would be only too happy to throw him to the wolves. Thank God he'd had the sense to realize it and stay away.

So he hadn't tried to contact Blix. He'd spent the day walking—stopping to rest at the little parks along the way.

He'd never realized how far it was from the Valley to Culver City, particularly when you have to make those uphill grades on foot. No wonder there aren't many pedestrians around anymore. The sun bakes the juices out of a man, and by the time you start downhill on the city side, you're tired and hungry and your throat is dust-dry.

That's what kept him going—his throat. Lorch turned away from the window and moved along the street.

There wasn't much traffic, not for early evening. Maybe everybody had decided to stay indoors tonight, because of what had happened. Well, he didn't blame them. But nothing they could have heard or read would ever begin to equal the reality. The way that nurse had looked when the cord tightened around her throat, the way Griswold screamed like a woman, the way he *smelled* when the current went on full force—

But he mustn't think about that now. He had to keep walking. Only a few blocks more. His feet burned, his throat burned, but he walked.

Nothing but business places here, no residences, and that was good. People who might recognize him were gone now, shops closed for the night. Lorch crossed the street—one more block to go, and he'd be home free. As far as he was concerned, the realty office was home. He couldn't consider going to the house; they'd be watching there for sure. But at this hour the office was probably safe. It better be, because he couldn't go much further.

There'd be some cash in the office; he kept

an electric razor there, and a change of clothing. Maybe even another pair of shoes, though he couldn't remember for sure. But once he had money in his pocket again he could make some plans.

Planning, that was his strong suit. Always had been. When you're a kid in an orphanage, you learn how to take care of yourself. And when you leave, you know how to make it on your own. You've found out the hard way that you don't need parents, so why worry about friends? It had been a long road he'd traveled from the orphanage to the Lorch Agency, and he'd made the trip alone. It was planning that kept him out of the draft, planning that got around the IRS and the Board of Realtors and all the other jokers who tried to stop him. *Tell 'em and sell 'em*—that was the big secret. If you tell the suckers what they want to hear, you can sell them what they don't want to buy. And that's why he'd ended up with his own company, the new Caddy every year, the monogrammed shirts, the forty-dollar haircuts, everything. Somewhere along the line he'd picked up this little drinking problem, but he had that under control, too. Nobody sent him to the sanatorium, he'd figured that move out for himself. And it worked. Plans always work.

Lorch started down the street, heading for

the office at the end of the block. Midway he passed the lights of the liquor store.

Funny, it hadn't been there a couple of months ago. Schermerhorn's property, wasn't it? Used to be a cycle shop, but vacant for a long time. He'd tried to get old man Schermerhorn to give him the listing, but the tight bastard turned him down—too cheap to pay commission. So he'd gone ahead and rented it on his own. *Mortlake Liquor* was the name, slashed across the storefront in red neon.

Lorch halted and glanced past the cardboard window displays, peering at the brightly lit interior beyond. He stared at aisle racks heaped with half-pints, counters cluttered with quarts, wall shelves filled with fifths, hosts of half-gallons, pyramids of pints.

The glittering reflection of light bounced off ten thousand bottles. It radiated from rum, glinted on gin, vivified vodka's crystal clarity. All the colors of the rainbow assaulted Lorch's eyes, and once again he was conscious of the burning in his throat.

Twenty-four hours without food will do that. Twenty-four hours without food, and two and a half months without a drink.

Lorch could see the proprietor sitting behind the counter next to the register. Little old man in a short-sleeved white shirt that hung down over his potbelly. You didn't have to look twice to know that he shuffled when he walked. And he wouldn't even have time to get to his feet if Lorch slipped through the doorway, grabbed a bottle from the nearest display and slipped out again. It would be easy.

Unless, of course, the old man had a gun under the counter. Or someone happened to come along just as he was on his way out. In any case, the old man would sound an alarm, and he'd have to run for it.

No, that wasn't the answer. He hadn't gone through two and a half months of purgatory and then the hell of last night just to start running. Not when he was so close to safety.

Just a few doors down was the realty office, and he'd find the answer there. The answer to his little drinking problem was in the big liquor cabinet behind his desk. *Little problem. Big cabinet.* Griswold said whiskey would kill him, but Griswold was a fool.

Lorch turned away, quickening his pace. *Not too fast now. Losing your grip, letting your mind go off like that. Because your throat burns. You still have to make plans.*

He came abreast of the frame bungalow set back from the street and turned down the walk. No sense going up to the front door; the lights were out—it was locked up for the night and he couldn't smash the lock, not here in full view of the street.

Lorch glanced around. No one in sight. He skirted the side of the bungalow, moving past the wooden sign on the lawn and into the shadows behind it. He emerged on an empty alleyway. There was a rear entrance, but Lorch didn't bother to try it; that door would be locked, too. His best bet was the window.

The window was around on the other side of the building. He moved up to it slowly, still conscious of the dryness in his throat. The window blinds were up, and he could stare into the darkness of his private office. He could see his desk, but not the liquor cabinet; it was in shadow. He knew it was there, though, and all that barred his way was a thin pane of glass. Easy enough to find a rock out in the alley—

No. Got to make plans. Lorch shook his head, taking a deep breath. Breaking glass was too noisy. If he could find something to pry the window open with—

Lorch extended his damp palms to test the frame. His hands were shaking now, he knew he'd have to hurry. His fingers slipped from the wood. The window was rising.

It was rising. It wasn't locked!

Goddam Blix and his efficiency. Smart operator and too dumb to remember to lock the window! Wait until he saw him, he'd chew him out—

Only he wasn't going to see Blix. That was the whole point. See no one. Take the money and walk, not run.

The window slid up.

Jack Lorch gripped the sill and hoisted himself to the ledge. Perspiration beaded his forehead, the rosary of effort. He sat panting there for a moment, eyes searching the alleyway, ears straining for sound. Darkness and silence reassured him, and his breathing subsided to a normal level. But his throat was dry. So dry—

Over the ledge and into the office. His desk loomed in the shadows. There was a desk lamp, but Lorch didn't turn it on. Too risky, and he didn't need light. He knew every foot of the office, every inch. He could find his way blind; the liquor cabinet was just five steps to the left on the wall behind the desk. All these miles, and now just five little steps to go.

Lorch groped along the side of the desk. The money would be in the upper righthand drawer. Loose change and a few small bills for petty cash, right on top. A metal box for checks and big bills. Locked, of course, but the key was always here, under the desk blotter. He could reach for it now, open the box—combination was forty left, fifty-seven right, twenty left—and put the money in his pocket. But that could wait for another minute. His pocket wasn't what burned.

First things first. First a drink, then the money, then plans. And maybe one more drink before the planning. That's the way he'd always worked, sitting behind the desk and relaxing over a shot while he figured the next move. And that's the way he'd work now. A drink, two drinks at most, but no more. Not on an empty stomach. And he wasn't going to slip back into the old routine again; he'd had it with alcoholism, he'd paid his dues. But that first one he needed. Now. To hell with Griswold and his oral-erotic crap, all that jive about infantile craving for the nipple. Once the cash was in his pocket he could have all the nipples in the world. Acres of tits, anything he wanted—after he had a drink.

Lorch stepped into the deeper shadow at the corner of the room. He moved faster than he realized; only four steps and he banged his forehead against the corner of the built-in liquor cabinet. He didn't hit hard, but the pain was just enough to sober him.

Sober. Funny word. Funny feeling. The way he felt now, opening the door of the liquor cabinet. Because he realized that up until now he'd been drunk. Dried out for two and a half months, but drunk as a lord. *Drunkenness is a state of mind*.

Of course. Why hadn't he figured that out before? Alcoholism doesn't come out of bottles, it comes out of craving. A few ounces deaden the pain of reality, but—by God, old Griswold told the truth!—the pain is subjective. Like all that crud going through his thoughts about the liquor store. An alcoholic is drunk before he ever starts drinking. He sets up his own crazy world, his thoughts are staggering long before his legs.

Lorch reached out and opened the door of the liquor cabinet, trying to focus his eyes on its contents.

There it was, three deep shelves crowded with bottles. Gin, vodka, vermouth, bitters on the bottom—Irish, Canadian, Scotch in the middle—top shelf, solid bourbon. Some of the bottles were partially empty, recapped and recorked, and he could smell their contents. The sharp reek penetrated his nostrils and curled down into his throat. Lorch found his hand automatically extending towards the top shelf, felt it falter and draw back as he realized his throat wasn't burning any longer.

Strange. All the dryness was gone, and he was conscious of another reaction. Gut-reaction. He was hungry. Not thirsty. He didn't need a drink. Oh, he wanted one all right, no sense trying to kid himself about that, but he didn't *need* it. What he needed was food. A good square meal. And then, he knew what to do.

A plan wasn't necessary. Now that he was sober, really sober, he knew it never had been necessary. Getting bombed and trying to fig- ure some way-out scheme for running off again—that had been the drunk's idea. But it wouldn't work, couldn't work. Where could he run to and how long before they'd catch up with him anyway? Sooner or later they'd find out he'd been involved; Blix would probably tell them after tonight and be a big hero.

So the thing to do was take the play away from Blix and call the police himself. Tell them exactly what had happened, lay it right on the line, name the others, cooperate. Sure, he'd have to clear his own part in it, and there'd be a lot of publicity. But it could be good publicity—good for him, good for the business. Simple, how everything fell into place once you stopped thinking drunk.

Standing there in the darkness, Lorch started to close the cabinet door. As he did so, he noticed there was a gap right in the middle of the top shelf. One of the bourbon bottles was missing. Blix didn't drink—who could have taken it?

The answer came out of the shadows behind him. Jack Lorch turned just in time to see the blurred motion of the bottle descending to smash his skull.

Then he fell, and the cabinet toppled forward and glass shattered on the floor and in his flesh. In the darkness blood and bourbon mingled and Lorch's thought—his last thought—was that Griswold had been right. It was liquor that killed him, after all.

CHAPTER 12

The man on night duty was named Lubeck. He arrived at Karen's apartment shortly before ten and had a little private conversation with Doyle outside in the hallway.

Then Doyle left and Lubeck took over. He was a few years older than his predecessor and a good twenty pounds heavier, but his very size and bulk seemed reassuring. Like Doyle, he made the rounds, checking closets and doors and windows.

"You intend to keep the air-conditioning on all night?" he asked. "Good. Then you won't be opening any windows." Lubeck walked back into the living room and adjusted the night chain on the door. Karen watched him from the bedroom.

"Mind if I use your phone?" he said. "I want to call in."

"Go right ahead."

Karen stood in the doorway as Lubeck dialed. She felt awkward coming back into the living room while he was phoning, but perhaps she could catch the conversation from where she was standing.

It didn't work out that way. Lubeck spoke very softly, and the air-conditioning drowned out his voice.

Karen shook her head. Why was she acting this way—afraid to walk into her own living room? She wasn't a prisoner.

Or was she?

A man in armor is his armor's slave. Robert Browning said that, in "Herakles." Why the quotation lingered in her mind all these years Karen had never known, but suddenly she realized it was true. We're all armored, and all enslaved. Just having Lubeck here made her a prisoner—a prisoner of her own need for protection. And Lubeck, armored with his badge and his service revolver, was a prisoner, too—the prisoner of a system that made him report to his superiors. And his superiors were prisoners of the politicians, and the politicians were the prisoners of the people, and the people were, like herself, serving a life sentence while trying to protect themselves against the world. Some of them, of course, were under a death sentence. And it could be carried out anytime—

Karen pushed the thought aside, forced herself to move forward from the doorway just as Lubeck replaced the phone in its cradle.

"Any news?"

Lubeck shook his head. "Nothing." He stood up. "But don't worry, everything's under control. They'll have a patrol car cruising the area all night. Which reminds me—"

"Yes?"

"I'll be reporting in a couple of times later on. So if you wake up and hear me on the phone, you'll know the reason."

"You're going to sit out here all night?"

"That's right. I won't bother you unless I have to. But keep your door open. And if you hear anything, give a holler." Lubeck smiled at her. "I know how you feel, it's a little embarrassing, but don't let it get you down."

"It doesn't," Karen lied.

"Oh, one thing more. You take anything

when you go to bed—any sedative, sleeping pills?"

"No."

"That's good."

Karen wasn't so sure, but she concealed her doubts. Right now she wanted something that would really knock her out. Undressing in the bathroom, she felt only too wide-awake, fully conscious of the stranger in the other room. She couldn't possibly fall asleep with him here—and on the other hand, she couldn't possibly fall asleep if he left. *A man in armor is his armor's slave.*

Karen took the spread off without turning on the bedroom light and crawled in under the sheet. She wouldn't be able to sleep but at least she could rest. The light from the living room filtered dimly along the hall. She closed her eyes against it, and went into the alpha cycle within thirty seconds after her head touched the pillow.

Somewhere in her dreams, Bruce appeared.

He was wearing armor and there was a sword in his hand.

A bloody sword.

CHAPTER 13

Louise Drexel heard it first.

Roger was in the study, working on his stamp collection, and she was in the library. Louise had always been fond of reading, and lately it seemed to occupy her time more and more. Theirs was probably the only house in Bel Air without a television set, and she really missed having one, but Roger was absolutely adamant. "Why stuff your ears with garbage?" he said, and she knew he felt very strongly about it, because he seldom used that sort of language. Louise was tempted to remind him that at one time he'd not only watched television but actually sponsored a program; it was only after he'd sold the business that he changed his mind. He stopped getting the newspaper, too, when he retired. "I'm sixty-five years old and entitled to a little peace and quiet," he told her. "We have enough troubles of our own without having to worry about other people's problems."

It was really Edna he was referring to when he talked about trouble, but neither of them wanted to discuss the matter any further. They'd done their best, and now it was up to the physicians. She was getting the very finest care and they could do no more. And after Roger's last attack there was simply no point in upsetting him by dwelling on unpleasant things. At first Louise had felt guilty about it—after all, Edna was her daughter, and one doesn't like to pretend that one's only child isn't a matter of concern—but then she reminded herself that her first duty was to her husband.

During his lengthy convalescence, they gave up entertaining and gradually lost touch with most of their friends. Since then neither of them had made any effort to renew social contacts. Again, it was because of Edna—no one outside of the doctor and the part-time help even suspected what had happened to her and where she was now, and it would be awkward to explain.

For a time Louise had felt lost and a bit lonely, but after a while she came to realize that Roger was right. The way things were today, it was better to deal with the world at one remove. As a philatelist, Roger collected little bits and pieces of the world and stuck them into books. As a reader, Louise extracted little bits and pieces of the world that would stick in her mind.

Tonight, for example, she was learning about Khumaraweh. He lived in a palace with walls of lapis lazuli and gold, surrounded by trees with trunks and branches coated in sheets of gilded copper, and he kept lions for pets. His favorite lion, Zouraik, had blue eyes. As a remedy for insomnia, Khumaraweh built an artificial lake, thirteen hundred feet square, in the palace garden, and filled it entirely with mercury. Here he slept on a mattress of inflated skins, lulled to slumber by the movement of the mercury.

It all sounded like something from a fairy tale, but she was reading history—Khumaraweh actually ruled in what has since become the city of Cairo, over eleven hundred years ago. And like Roger, all he desired was peace and quiet.

Louise had just started on the section of the book describing Khumaraweh's room of golden statues when the peace and quiet was shattered by the sound.

The noise wasn't loud, but it was persistent, and it seemed to be coming from the rear of the house. Louise's first thought was that a shutter might be banging against one of the kitchen windows.

Frowning, Louise put her book aside and made her way along the hall.

Even before she entered the kitchen, she could see that the window-shutters were firmly secured. The noise was someone pounding on the back door.

Louise wondered if she ought to get the gun—everyone in the neighborhood kept a gun in the house, ever since those movie people down the street had been robbed—but the revolver was in a desk drawer in the study, and she'd have to disturb Roger. *No excitement,* the doctor had said.

Louise hesitated. The door was locked and bolted. Perhaps if she just picked up the phone very quietly and called the police—

The pounding became a frantic hammering. And above it, Louise heard the voice.

"Let me in! Let me in—"

Quickly, Louise crossed the room and fumbled with the bolt and key.

She opened the door and Edna fell into her arms.

"Mama—" She was panting, sobbing, her hair stringy and disheveled, her face grimy and streaked with tears.

"What happened?"

Edna looked up and shook her head. Then she turned swiftly and closed the kitchen door. As Louise watched, she locked the door again, slid the bolt fast, moved to the wall switch and extinguished the outside lights for the patio and pool.

As she did so, Louise realized what Edna was wearing—it was just a soiled smock of some sort, with absolutely nothing underneath. There were sandals on her stockingless feet, and ridges of swollen flesh puffed and protruded between the thongs. Her sunburned forehead was raw and red.

Edna nodded. "Quick, get me out of here before he comes—"

Louise put out her hand. "Wait. You father is in the study. He's been very ill. We mustn't alarm him."

"I'm not alarmed."

Louise turned. Roger was standing in the hall doorway, staring at them. He seemed quite calm.

"Daddy?" Edna wasn't calm. She began to sob again, moving towards Roger, arms outstretched.

Roger stepped back. "None of that," he said. "You're a grown woman, Edna. You're forty-two years old. I think you owe your mother and me an explanation for all this—"

It sounded cold, it sounded cruel, but Louise knew what he was doing, and why. *You've got to stop treating her like a child*, Dr. Griswold had said. *It's the only way to halt her retreat into these fantasies.*

Of course Dr. Griswold had said a great deal more, but Louise could hardly accept all that. All she and Roger had ever done was to try and protect the girl from harmful outside influences, keeping her away from bad companions and seeing to it that she didn't fall into the hands of some fortune hunter. The idea that all these years of careful shielding were actually the cause of paranoid symptoms was obviously absurd, and what Griswold said about sexual repression was downright indecent. Still, there was no denying Edna's need for treatment, and Dr. Griswold came highly recommended for his discretion.

"Suppose you tell us just what happened," Roger was saying.

Edna shook her head. "He might hear—"

Louise started to reply, but Roger's look

silenced her. "We'll go to the study," he said. He turned and led the way down the hall.

Edna was limping badly, Louise noticed, but she seemed to be controlling herself; the disturbing facial tic she'd had during the last months before going to the sanatorium was gone now. And in the study, when she sank into the big chair, she looked like a child in her oversized gown—a frightened child, with gray in her hair.

"Can I get you something, dear?" Louise asked. "A glass of milk—"

"No, Mama."

Louise stared at her daughter's feet. "At least let me help you take those sandals off." She started forward, but Roger stepped in front of her. He smiled down at Edna.

"First things first," he said. "Before we go into anything else, I want you to know that your mother and I are glad to see you home again."

"Are you?"

"Of course. I'm sure you understand that our only concern is for your welfare. You do know that, don't you?"

"Yes." Edna's voice was faint and she didn't look at him.

"Good." Roger nodded approval. "Then you must realize that we arranged your stay in the sanatorium because the doctor said it was the only way to help you. And you were helped there, weren't you?"

"Yes, Daddy."

Roger's smile never faltered. "Then why did you run away?" he said.

Edna glanced up quickly. "I didn't run away! They took me—"

"Who took you?"

"The others. I had to go with them, I couldn't stay there alone after what happened! We went in Dr. Griswold's car, last night—"

"And he let you go?"

Edna shook her head. "Dr. Griswold is dead."

Roger wasn't smiling now. He frowned at Louise, then faced his daughter. "Go on," he said softly.

And Edna went on, but not softly. As she spoke, her voice honed itself to a hysterical edge, cutting through all composure.

Listening, Louise remembered the screams and the raving she'd heard before they took Edna away. During the long months those screams had faded to faint echoes, and even Edna's image had paled to a ghostly presence which haunted her only in troubled sleep. Now, once again, the voice was real and Edna was real. But what she was saying—

Dr. Griswold was dead, the night nurse was dead, Herb Thomas the orderly was dead, too. He had planned it, he killed them, and now he said they would all be free. And he took the car and told them he'd drive them into town, take them wherever they wanted, but he stopped somewhere in the Valley. He'd made them stay in the car while he went off, first giving Tony a gun and telling him to keep them there until he came back. That was when Edna knew he was lying, he wouldn't ever let them go, he would kill them all. The others seemed to know it too, because they started to fight with Tony in the back seat. So she jumped out of the car and started to run, hiding at night on the way up Beverly Glen and then coming down by the side roads into Bel Air today. She would have been here sooner except that by noon she began to have this feeling that she was being followed, and she knew he was coming after her. So she had to wait until dark and move very slowly, because if he ever caught up with her—

"Who?" Roger said. "What's his name?"

"I—I don't know his name."

"You don't know?"

Edna shook her head. Her eyes darted to the drawn drapes on the windows. "He could be out there now," she whispered. "If he heard me tell, he'd kill you, too."

"But that's ridiculous—" Louise checked herself as Roger shot her a warning glance.

Edna huddled up as though she was trying

to hide in the big wing chair. "His eyes," she said. "I can feel his eyes. Like knives stabbing. He's crazy, you know. The rest of them, they're just sick, but he's really crazy. He can look at people and make them do whatever he wants. That's why Tony helped him. He even had Dr. Griswold fooled. He can look at you and tell just what you're thinking. He burned everything up in the fireplace, but first he found out where all of us lived, so if we got away, he could come after us. Because he doesn't want anybody to know. If he ever finds me—"

Her left cheek began to twitch; the tic was back. Roger went over and put his hand on her shoulder.

"He won't find you," he said. "I promise."

"Maybe we can run away," Edna said. "We could go away right now in your car."

"That's an idea." Roger turned to Louise. "Take her upstairs and get her some decent clothes. She can't travel like this."

"But, Roger—"

"Do as I say." He winked quickly. "I'll join you in a moment."

Roger turned, smiled at Edna, and went out into the hall. A moment later, Louise heard the sound of the library door closing softly.

"All right, Edna," Louise said. "Let's go."

Edna shook her head. "No."

"What's the matter?"

"He didn't believe me."

"Of course he believed you." Louise reached down and took hold of Edna's wrist. Her hand was filthy and the nails had been bitten to the quick. Louise could feel the pulse jumping as she pulled Edna to her feet. "Please," she said. "We've got to hurry and get ready to leave when your father joins us."

"Do you believe me, Mama?"

"Yes." Louise led her daughter to the doorway. "Now, come along. You'll have a nice hot shower, and then we'll pick out a pretty dress for you." Louise kept talking, raising her voice as she moved down the hall past the library door to distract Edna's attention. "You remember that lovely new outfit you got just before you went away? Well, it's still in your closet—I've kept all your things spic-and-span—"

Behind the closed door of the library she could hear Roger's muffled voice on the telephone. "—emergency. Get me the police—"

Edna's hand jerked free. For a moment Louise was taken by surprise; all she could think of was how strong Edna was. And then she felt that strength explode against her temple, felt her head snap back against the wall, felt—nothing.

When Louise finally came to, she looked up

and saw Roger bending over her, shaking her shoulder. As her vision cleared, the figure behind him came into focus, blue uniform and all.

"Police—here already?" she murmured.

"I've been trying to bring you to for fifteen minutes," Roger said. "Easy—don't move!"

"I'm all right." Louise felt a pounding as she sat up, a sickening throbbing spreading from the spot where the back of her head had struck the wall. But they helped her to her feet and she found she was able to stand. Roger put his arm around her shoulders.

"Where's Edna?" she said.

No one answered. It wasn't necessary; when Louise glanced down the hall into the kitchen beyond, she could see the open door leading out to the grounds at the rear of the house. All the floodlights were on, and in the distance other figures in blue uniforms were moving back and forth beside the swimming pool. Louise blinked to clear her blurring vision.

"She heard you and ran away," Louise murmured. "Why don't they go after her?" She tried to wrench free from Roger's arm, but he held her firmly.

"Don't go out there," he said.

It wasn't necessary to go out there, because the men in the blue uniforms were coming in, moving very slowly, and Louise saw what they were carrying. And now everything was very clear, as clear as the drops of water which fell from the soaking white gown, the hanging, stringy hair.

Edna. She'd run out in a blind panic. She'd fallen into the pool—drowned—

For a moment Louise thought she was going to pass out again. But they wouldn't let her look at the body, they made her go back into the study and lie down, and Roger gave her some brandy.

It wasn't until later that they told her Edna hadn't fallen into the pool. They'd found her lying beside it, with only the upper portion of her body hanging down submerged over the edge. Even though her head was under water, she hadn't died of drowning.

Edna had been strangled.

CHAPTER 14

On Sunset Strip the vibes were good.

At the porno theatre the skin-flick buffs were lining up for the midnight show—a nudie film featuring the misadventures of an Indian girl named Split Beaver.

Down the street, the outdoor tables of the hamburger joints were crowded with customers partaking of both hamburgers and joints.

And on the corner of Laurel Canyon Boulevard, Tony Rodell stood statue-still, blowing his mind. He was into everything and everything was outta sight.

The bumper sticker on the dune buggy with its neat lettering, *Scrou Yew*.

The dude in the Christian Dior tank-top, screaming at his companion—"How could a boy like you fall in love with Ronald? Why, he's old enough to be your mother!"

The chick with the Afro yelling to someone on the sideway, "Come over on Saturday for the Black Mass. We're having it catered."

Oh wow!

This is where it was at and it was good to be back. The biggest light show on earth, action everywhere you looked; the whole street filled with midnight cowboys, and looking down on the scene from the oversized painted billboards, the hairy-glary faces of the gods themselves: The Up Yours, The Wall-To-Wall Sewer, Stockyard Slim and The Pigs.

Last year Tony had been on the boards himself. That was when the record came out and the group was set to play Tahoe. Then everything went down the tubes, they busted the gig the first night, and his own mother—his own frigging mother—gave him the shaft.

It had been a real rip-off, and at first Tony had psyched out on the whole scene. It wasn't until after that he realized she must have known about the bust in advance and made a deal; she'd finger the group if they dropped charges on him. But the only way the fuzz would go for it would be if she promised to keep him clean. That's why the old lady put him on ice at the san. Shred a lot of bread to stash him away there, and if she and Griswold had their way he'd probably be playing with himself forever, or at least until the loot ran out.

But something else had run out for Griswold before the loot did, and he wasn't going back. No way. His hair was short now and the beard was gone; his own mother wouldn't recognize him. Not until it was too late—

Late. It was past midnight, and nobody'd showed.

Tony shifted his feet and then his gaze, scanning the oncoming traffic along Sunset. Twelve o'clock across from Schwab's, that's what the man had said, and he'd been standing here for over twenty minutes. The vibes were getting bad now, and he remembered last night's conversation.

It was after the man came back to the parked car and found everybody had split and Tony lying across the back seat, knocked out with the butt of the gun he was supposed to keep them all covered with. The man slapped Tony until he came around, and for a minute Tony was uptight because he had seen what the man could do when he got angry.

"I couldn't help it," Tony kept saying. "They all jumped me at once. If you'd only let me put the goddam bullets in the gun—"

"So you could blast somebody and bring the heat down on us?" The man sighed. He gave Tony one of those weirdo looks and then he said one of those weirdo things. "How do I hate thee? Let me count the ways." And laughed his weirdo laugh, which meant everything was all right. "Don't worry, I didn't expect to keep them together much longer. Maybe it will even be easier now that they've cut out—unless one of them gets picked up before."

"Before what?" Tony said.

But the man just laughed again and put the gun in his pocket. "Leave it to me. Now let's get moving."

"Want me to drive?"

The man shook his head. "We're ditching the car here."

"Why?"

"For the same reason I'm going to get rid of this." And he patted the pocket with the gun in it. "From now on, we cover our trail. Good military strategy, as von Clausewitz would say."

"Von who?"

142

"Friend of mine." The man helped Tony sit up and climb out of the car. "You look all right," he said. "Think you can walk?"

"Sure. I was just stunned for a minute."

"Good. Then start walking."

"Aren't you coming with me?"

The man shook his head. "He travels the fastest who travels alone." He kept looking at Tony, and you could almost see the gears turning inside his head. Tony wondered whether anybody had ever gotten inside his head; maybe Griswold. But Griswold had been chewed up in the machinery, and Tony wasn't about to go that route. "Tomorrow night," the man said. And that's when he made the date.

"But why can't I stick with you?" Tony asked.

"Negative. Suppose somebody does get picked up and describes us? It's hard to slap a make on anyone from just a verbal description—but when you've got two people together and two identifications to go on, it's a lot easier. Besides, I've got things to do."

"You mean I'm supposed to hang loose for twenty-four hours?"

"No. You're going to hang tight." The man gave him some bills—probably from old Griswold's wallet. "Go to a motel, get some rest. Grab yourself something to eat tomorrow, but stay indoors as much as possible until dark."

143

"Why in hell not just head for my pad?"

"Because if the fuzz does get the word, that's the first place they'll look for you. We'll wait until we're sure there's no heat."

"And then what?"

"Don't worry. Have I ever let you down?"

Both of them knew the answer to that one. If it hadn't been for the man and his plan, Tony would still be doing couch-time in Shrink City. But he'd listened to the man, and that's what had brought him this far; might as well go all the way.

So the man walked west and Tony walked east, holing up in a raunchy little motel over on Ventura where nobody worried about luggage; like the man, he was wearing civvy threads instead of a patient's gown, and that helped.

Sleeping didn't come easy, not with all the pictures that popped into Tony's head the minute he closed his eyes; he hadn't seen Griswold or the nurse, but he'd watched Herb die. It was pretty bad the first time, and the rerun wasn't any better, except that Tony kept reminding himself that it was all over. And there was no sense worrying about the others; they'd be just as hot to get away as he was, and play it just as cool. The man knew what he was doing, and he always kept his word. He said they'd crash out, and they'd crashed; now he said they'd make it the rest of the way, and they would.

Along towards dawn Tony managed to fall asleep, and when morning came, he felt better. Today he'd hopped a bus down to Hollywood Boulevard and lost himself in one of the continuous-performance movie houses, seeing a double feature. In the first picture, the blue-clad, middle-aged U.S. Cavalry disemboweled innocent young redskins; in the second, the blue-clad middle-aged cops disemboweled innocent young rioters. Right on, until after dark; then Tony had just enough left for a couple of hot dogs at a Boulevard stand. It wasn't such a good idea, because the hot-dog casings reminded him a little of the intestines he'd seen hanging out in the films, but of course those were only movies, and GP-rated at that. Nobody rated the hot dogs.

Then Tony started to walk up the Boulevard, past the windows of the bookshops *(Historic Privies Of The Old West)* and the record stores *(1971's Oldies But Goodies).* He wondered idly if his disc was still in stock, but decided against going inside and looking around. Better keep moving.

Keep moving, past the straights sniffing around the forecourt of Grauman's Chinese ("Look, Mom—is that a real hippie?") and down La Brea to Sunset, and then along Sunset itself past the organic-food hangouts for the health freaks and the gay bars. And then onto the Strip, the other side of Fairfax, and here he was, and where the hell was the man?

Somebody honked a car horn, and Tony turned his head, recognizing the sound. As well he might, because he recognized the car, too. It was his own MG, and the man was behind the wheel, angling over to the curb in the right-lane traffic.

"Hurry," said the man, which was ridiculous, because everyone had stopped for the light anyway.

Tony hopped in, and when the light changed, the MG turned and started up Laurel Canyon.

"Hey, man, where'd you get my wheels?" he said.

The man smiled. "From those wonderful folks who brought you the Crucifixion."

He was wearing a new outfit—dark jacket and slacks. Courtesy of Griswold's wallet, Tony figured. And his smile told him that everything was copasetic.

"You hit my pad," Tony said.

The man nodded. "Wanted to check it out, make sure we wouldn't have problems."

"What about fuzz?"

"If ignorance is bliss, they're the happiest people on earth."

"Nobody blew the whistle?"

146

"Not a living soul." The man pulled up at the Hollywood Boulevard intersection, then gunned forward as the green signal came. "Quite a place you've got."

"I told you it was groovy."

"Somehow I didn't expect all that much elegance. At some point the architect must have decided to risk everything and go for baroque."

"Used to belong to a producer. Business manager picked it up cheap last year. He said it was a good deal."

"He's the one who's been looking after it for you?"

"No. We cooled the contract when I went to the san. My old lady comes by a couple of times a week. Keeps the car battery going, cleans the joint up, sees that the dogs get fed." Tony grinned. "How about those dogs?"

"Scared the living Jesus out of me. They started barking when I went over the wall, and I almost changed my mind." The man wheeled over to the left-turn lane at Lookout Mountain. "Good thing she keeps them chained."

"You've got to, with Dobermans. But guard dogs are a good idea, up in the hills. Of course both of them know me, and they're used to my old lady, too, but any stranger comes around—look out!"

"They kept howling all the time I was in

the house. Figured they were hungry, so I got a can of dog food from the kitchen and took it out to them. But believe me, I didn't get too close."

"When they see us together, they won't give you any trouble. Like I say, they're just like puppies with me and my old lady."

The MG was climbing up Lookout now, past Horseshoe Canyon to the school, then taking the fork-off on Wonderland Avenue. Even in the darkness the route was familiar to Tony, and suddenly, for the first time, he had this coming-home feeling. He realized how much he'd been missing being in his own pad, seeing Tiger and Butch.

"You say your mother stops by several times a week?" the man asked.

"Don't worry, she won't be around again until Thursday."

"How do you know?"

"I told you—she called the san day before yesterday. Said she was going to Vegas for a couple of days."

"What if she taps out? Wouldn't she come back earlier?"

"She doesn't go there for the action. When there's a big convention at the Flamingo, she runs up and works the tables. Cocktail waitress." Tony nodded. "Look at her, you'd never figure she had a grown son. Why, a couple of years ago, over on Western, she was working topless."

"I saw a real topless waitress once," the man said.

"Real topless?"

"That's right." The man smiled. "Somebody had cut off her head."

Tony smiled, too, even though the gag was old. Or was it a gag? With this cat you never knew. One minute he was making funnies, the next he was rapping philosophy. But he was the one who could put it all together, and that's what counted.

The MG turned onto Wonderland Park, still climbing. The road was narrower here, and darker; the higher you went, the narrower and darker it got. No yard lights, no lights in the hillside houses. Hard to believe it was only ten minutes' driving from here to the Strip. Living up here, you were really hiding out. Most of the time you were above the smog and it was usually a lot cooler than down below. The people were cool, too. That's why Tony went for it in the first place.

It would be good to be home again, even for a little while. Only for a little while, of course, because once the fuzz got organized, there'd be too much heat from below.

Tony glanced at his companion. "What happens next?" he asked.

"I've got a few ideas about that. Wait until we get inside where we can relax."

Tony noticed that the MG was crawling along in low now, making the turns that led up to the house at the very top almost in slow-motion. And the man was keeping an eye on every shadow, every parked car, making sure no one was watching, no one was waiting. A damn good thing, too; this was no time to start talking about futures. Play it by ear.

Now his ear told him that the dogs had heard the car coming. They were growling behind the wall. The MG pulled up in front of the driveway and halted, motor running.

The man reached into his jacket pocket and tossed a keychain into Tony's lap. "You won't have to go over the wall," he said. "I found these inside your desk."

Tony opened the door and slid out. He could hear Tiger and Butch whining and sniffling, hear their claws scratching and scraping the wall as they got excited. Well, he was excited, too; just seeing the house was enough after all this time. He must have missed it more than he'd known.

Tony glanced at the man. He still sat behind the wheel. "Aren't you coming in?"

"Not until I put the car in the garage. Somebody sees it parked on the street tomorrow, they might get ideas."

Good thinking. Tony circled his approval with thumb and forefinger, and the man nodded.

"You go ahead in and see if you can keep those dogs quiet."

Tony walked over to the gate and opened it. Even the feel of the key turning in the lock was somehow comforting and familiar.

He moved inside the patio, closing the gate behind him as the dogs snarled. Over the noise he heard the sound of the MG's motor, revving up and pulling away. But before he could think about it, Tony turned and saw Tiger and Butch. To his surprise, they were unchained, and they were racing towards him, fangs bared and dripping, red eyes glaring in the moonlight. Then the moonlight was blotted out as they leaped. Tony screamed and turned, but it was too late.

CHAPTER 15

The earth rotates on its axis in four minutes less than twenty-four hours. It orbits around the sun at approximately eighteen and a half miles per second, while at the same time whirling through space at a speed of more than ten thousand miles an hour.

Lieutenant Franklyn Barringer accepted all this because the scientists said it was so. Accepted, but did not truly believe.

Sitting behind his desk with both feet firmly

on the floor, he could not completely comprehend he was actually spinning around in a circle on a ball that was simultaneously revolving around another sphere at a dizzying pace, while at the same time whizzing up or down or sideways. And yet, he told himself, *it's happening, it's a demonstrable fact even if it seems incredible.* So one accepts the evidence and dismisses it.

The trouble is, there's some evidence, equally incredible, which can't be disposed of so easily. Such as the portfolio accumulating on Barringer's desk this morning; the memos of phone calls, the taped transcriptions, the reports.

"All right," he muttered. "So I've got to accept it. I still can't believe—"

"And you want me to convince you, is that right?" said Dr. Vicente.

"Not necessarily." Barringer poured himself a cup of coffee. "You've gone over this stuff. I want your opinion."

"In other words, an educated guess." Vicente reached for the coffee urn and refilled his own cup. "To begin with, could one man possibly commit all of these murders within the space of about four hours? Under certain conditions, the answer is a qualified yes."

"What are the conditions?"

"That he had the names and addresses of

the victims—which he could have obtained, either from them directly, or from Griswold's files before he burned them. That he had the means of transportation—and we know from the tire-marks at the house he was driving Tony Rodell's car, or at least a car which had occupied Rodell's garage. Lastly, that he had some reasonable assurance these people would be turning up at their homes or places of business at various times yesterday evening—"

"Edna Drexel told her parents they scattered in all directions out in Sherman Oaks."

"She also said she felt someone was following her."

"You forgot—only two hours earlier, Jack Lorch was killed in Culver City."

"From Culver City to Bel Air is only a half hour's drive."

"But how did he know Edna Drexel would be going home?"

"For the same reason he knew he'd find Jack Lorch at his office. These people had nowhere else to go. No money, no food."

"Sounds as if he was pushing his luck."

"He didn't have any choice in the matter. I think originally he planned to dispose of them *en masse*, that night when he had them all together in Griswold's car. Again, according to the Drexel woman's story, Tony Rodell was holding them all at gun-point. He might have intended to drive the whole group up to Rodell's house and finish them off there, with Rodell's help. But when they made a break for it, he had to track them down individually and take his chances."

"You keep saying 'he.' Don't forget, there's two men still at large."

"I know. But one of them was part of the group that ran off. And he's still hiding somewhere, unless our man got to him, too, and we haven't heard about it yet."

"We don't know a damned thing, except that two men are loose somewhere, and one of them is named Bruce Raymond. He's either the killer or a potential victim. Take your choice."

Vicente gulped coffee, then set his mug down on the desk top. "From what we know about Raymond, he could be either. I read that report from the VA. Marked instability, but cooperative, responsive to therapy—a lot of cautious phrases, all of which adds up to a lame excuse for releasing him and giving his bed to another patient. No definite prognosis, just something to protect the doctor making the decision."

"Who handled his case out there?"

"A Major Fairchild. I tried to contact him yesterday, but he's long gone. They had an address in Seattle—something called the Trade

Clinic—but when I phoned, I was told he'd left for a vacation in Japan. You could probably reach him through—"

"No time." Barringer shook his head. "And even if we did, how the hell is some army medico in Japan going to tell us if one of his former patients might have gone berserk here?"

"He can't, and neither can I." Dr. Vicente pushed his chair back. "But I can tell you something about the type of man who did commit these killings."

"Another educated guess?"

"Not entirely. We've got certain facts to go on. Number One, as I told you, he's undoubtedly a sociopath—"

"Can you give it to me without the psychiatric jargon?"

"Okay, no cautious phrases." Vicente smiled, then sobered. "To repeat what we already know, our man isn't recognizable as a nut. He looks and behaves like a rational human being. It's an act, of course, but a convincing one—we know that because he managed to organize his whole break from the sanatorium without arousing the suspicions of the staff or his fellow patients. In fact, he was able to get the other patients to accompany him. He's probably accustomed to taking over, to giving orders—"

"Raymond was an officer."

"Noted." Vicente nodded. "Another thing. From the nature of the crimes, we must assume we're dealing with someone who has great physical strength. Even if we accept Tony Rodell as his accomplice, it's apparent that force was involved as well as the element of surprise. Griswold was strapped into a chair, Jack Lorch was struck over the head, an orderly stabbed, two women strangled, Dorothy Anderson's throat was cut—"

"That's another thing that bothers me," Barringer said. "Each killing was different. Usually there's a pattern."

"We're not dealing with a compulsive murderer. There's no fetishism, apparently, no overt sadomasochistic component." Vicente paused, aware of his lapse into forensic phraseology. "On the conscious level, this man is killing merely to cover his tracks, using whatever means is practical at the moment. On the unconscious level, of course, it's another story. Anyone who would plan the kind of death meted out to Tony Rodell—"

"We don't know that he planned it," Barringer interrupted. "It could have been accidental. Granted, those Dobermans were vicious, but they knew their master."

"So do we." Dr. Vicente riffled through the papers on Barringer's desk. "You talked to his mother this morning."

"And got absolutely nothing." Barringer shook his head. "Aside from identifying her son as one of the missing patients, everything she told us was an obvious falsehood. Tony was a good boy, maybe a little disturbed, but no real problems."

"She's the victim's mother. What do you expect her to say under the circumstances?"

"It doesn't matter. We've got his record." This time it was Barringer who pawed through the documents on the desk until he found a sheet and scanned it. "High school dropout. Stolen-vehicle charge at sixteen, suspended and probation. His mother swears he was always clean, but we've got two counts here involving narcotics."

"Before or after he organized his rock group?"

"After. Apparently he was making it big in music—big enough to buy that house and maintain it. I got the mother to admit she hadn't seen her son for almost a year before he went into the sanatorium, but she refused to talk about the commitment. I think he went in because he was hooked. Freaked out on speed."

"Any reason to support that theory?"

"Two thousand reasons." Barringer took a last gulp of coffee. "Two bottles, each containing a thousand amphetamine capsules, stashed away under the meat packages in the freezer. Turned up this morning when they went through the house. One of the bottles sealed, the other open."

Dr. Vicente's eyes narrowed. "What does that suggest to you?"

"That Rodell and the murderer arrived at the house together, possibly planning to spend the night there. They probably had Rodell's car—for all we know, they'd been together during the evening, when the murders were committed."

"You think Tony Rodell was involved in the slayings?"

"Could be. Particularly if he'd located his supply of capsules earlier, when they came to pick up the car. I don't have to tell you what a speed freak is capable of when he's really turned on." Barringer shifted his empty coffee mug on the desk top. "Let's say he was still high when they returned to the house, really flying. High enough to mistreat those dogs. They attacked him, and his companion got scared, took off in the car."

"Any evidence that the dogs were mistreated? Did your people turn up a stick, or a whip at the scene?"

"No, nothing but a wrapper from one of the meat packages. Perhaps he was just teasing the dogs, showing them the meat and then snatching it away, that sort of thing." Barringer shrugged. "When you're dealing with a speed freak, anything's possible."

"Let's stick to what's probable," Dr. Vicente said. "You say there's no pattern in these slayings. What you really mean is there's no consistency of *method*. But the pattern is plainly visible in the *motive*. One by one, the murderer is killing all the people who could identify him. We both agree that Tony Rodell could have identified the murderer. Which makes his death part of the pattern."

"How did the murderer get those dogs to attack Rodell?"

"I don't know." Dr. Vicente stood up. "Any more than you really know whether or not Rodell was under the influence of amphetamine at the time of his death."

"But I'm going to find out." Barringer frowned and reached for the telephone.

Dr. Vicente was silent as the Lieutenant put through a call to the deputy coroner's office. The conversation that followed was cryptic, but Barringer's expression, when he cradled the phone again, told its own story.

"Okay, Doc," he said. "The p.m.'s not completed, but preliminaries on Rodell's blood samples and stomach contents show he was clean when he died."

"No trace of amphetamine?"

Barringer shook his head. "Not in Rodell.

But you were right—the dogs didn't attack him by accident. They'd been fixed."

"Fixed?"

"The dogs were destroyed this morning. I asked for an examination. According to the report, their stomachs were full of meat—and indications are that they were fed at least half a dozen capsules along with it.

"No wonder they attacked Rodell when he came in. They would have attacked anything that moved. Somebody turned those dogs on with speed."

CHAPTER 16

He spent the night in the car, parked inside the barricaded cul-de-sac of an abandoned freeway entrance. Shrubbery shielded him from the street as he slept.

Sleeping was never a problem; he merely closed his eyes and fell immediately into a dark hole. A hiding place, lightless and soundless, where nothing could find him, not even a dream. He hadn't dreamed in years.

"Of course you dream," the doctor always

insisted. "Everyone dreams. It's just that you repress such memories from your consciousness." The implication was obvious; he was blocking out recall because his nightmares were too terrible to be borne. That's what the doctor wanted to believe, but he was wrong. Nothing is too terrible to be borne. He had proved that beyond a doubt—not in dreams, but in reality. No one had ever suffered as he suffered, and yet he had survived. He survived, and the others—the dreamers—were dead. As for himself, he merely slept. Slept snugly, slept securely, slept with the certainty of one who knows he will awaken. *For I am the resurrection and the life, forever and ever. Amen.*

Awakening came with a rumble and a roar.

He blinked into instantaneous awareness, scrambling up out of the dark hole as the bombs fell—*no, not bombs, that was in another time, another place.*

Then he knew where he was, here in the cul-de-sac, and he recognized the source of the sound: garbage trucks, moving into the early-morning emptiness of the street in line of duty. Immediately upon realizing what he was hearing his heart stopped pounding and he was calm again.

He sat up, permitting himself a slight smile,

not in acknowledgment of the content of his thought, but in appreciation of the discipline and control which enabled him to evolve it so effortlessly. How many others, under similar circumstances, could come up with something like that?

No one else could. Because there were no others, not really. They were only actors. Of course none of them knew it, any more than the doctor did. They thought they were real, but they were only figments of imagination. *The world is my idea.*

It was discovering this secret which made everything so easy.

At first he hadn't been certain. He'd wondered what it would be like, wondered if he could actually carry out the part he had rehearsed over and over again in his mind. He had written the play, directed it, blocked out the movements, selected the cast, planned the whole production. He knew his own role perfectly, but the nagging doubt had remained— could he play it?

Now he knew the answer. There had been no stage fright. *Grand Guignol,* Theatre of Cruelty, call it what you will, was no different from the Theatre of the Absurd. Comedy and Tragedy alike were only masks to be worn and discarded at will. One had only to remember that it was all make-believe. The blood was merely ketchup, the twitching and grimaces and shrieks and cries all emanated from actors responding on cue, hamming it up for their big death scene.

Of course he had to be careful, because *he* was real, and his blood wasn't ketchup. Everyone would be crying, "Author, author!" but he couldn't afford to take bows; he had to avoid the spotlight at all costs. The best way was to keep changing roles.

Each man in his time plays many parts. The dutiful-patient character for Dr. Griswold and the staff; the all-powerful leader for the other patients. And then, for select audiences of one, the silent bits. The man in the closet for Dorothy Anderson, the man in the shadows for Jack Lorch, the man in the garden waiting for Edna Drexel. The swimming pool had been a great prop; something stirring in his memory told him he'd plagiarized it from that old Oriental melodrama, *Kismet.* Life copies art.

But Tony Rodell's removal from the stage had been a matter of brilliant improvisation. Using the dogs that way had been a stroke of genius; perhaps he'd managed to fool the audience completely.

He leaned forward in the car seat and switched on the radio, then push-buttoned his way across the dial in search of the early morning news.

The announcer's chatter gave him the answer he was seeking.

"—shocking and brutal series of murders climaxed in the early hours of this morning by the death of former rock-and-pop music star Tony Rodell—"

He listened until he was satisfied they'd found out about the dogs; that was important. They hadn't found out about him, and that was more important still. The rest was merely an exercise in ill-tempered name-calling—"homicidal maniac still on the loose," and all the rest of it. People who don't understand the play always give it bad notices.

He switched off the radio and plugged in the shaver he'd picked up in the drugstore yesterday. Using the rearview mirror, he removed the bristle of beard from his face. Then he reached under the seat and brought out a change of clothing. Lucky there'd been so much cash in Griswold's wallet, enough for a fresh outfit. He remembered how careful he'd been with Dorothy Anderson—actually taking one of the smocks hanging in her closet and tying it around his neck like an apron to protect himself from the spattering blood. He'd tossed the stained smock into a gully before picking up Tony Rodell's car and they apparently hadn't found it yet—not that the smock would be of any help to them.

He peered through the bushes at the street beyond. Some morning traffic was passing—people on their way to work—but nobody glanced his way. Even so, he slid down behind the wheel, concealing himself as much as possible as he shed his old garments and donned the new. Just his luck to be picked up for indecent exposure.

No, it wasn't just his luck. *His* luck was good, had been from the beginning. Because the wise man makes his own luck, and he had everything worked out.

He slipped the trousers on, then picked the pins out of the new shirt. Once he'd buttoned it, he reached for the necktie and sat upright in the seat again as he knotted it, eyes intent on the mirror. Then he transferred the contents of his pockets to the new outfit, pausing to count the money remaining in Griswold's wallet. Thirty-four dollars. Not a fortune, but enough to carry him through the day. And there would be more money. More money, and more days.

For the first time he permitted the thought to openly intrude. It had been waiting there for some time, waiting patiently until the stage was set. *Why limit this to one performance?*

Even at the sanatorium, he had sensed the notion. And last night it had made itself felt even more strongly. Now, today, he would reach the climax and the curtain would fall. His part would be over.

But did it have to end?

Eliminating witnesses was conceived of as a precautionary measure, and that made sense. But why stop there?

The world was full of candidates for oblivion. Like that ass on the radio, with his self-righteous braying about a "homicidal maniac." Yes, and so many others.

A parade began to pass through his mind, led by a leggy, half-naked drum majorette, smirking and strutting in hot pants, fondling the silver phallus beloved by all such teasing bitches, licking her lips as she jabbed it up into the air in mockery of a man's role. After her, the idiot cheerleader, breasts bobbing beneath her sweater, cavorting with grotesque grimaces and spastic gestures as she shrieked passionately, "Gimme a *P*, gimme a *U*, gimme a *K*, gimme an *E*!!" And then, burly, brawny, bulging brute in uniform, face of a fish fast-frozen, eyes like marbles, body moving mindlessly in the stiff-gaited rhythm of a robot—His Militant Majesty, the drill sergeant, barking incessantly and insanely the meaningless distillation of all stupidity, "Ten-*hut!*"

And behind him, all the others, the millions upon millions of others, who followed such leaders. Who accepted the orotund obscenities of the announcers and the lewd lies they burbled about people they'd never seen and products they'd never used. Who applauded the drum majorettes as "cute," as part of the spectacle of "good, clean sports," performed by lumbering cretins kicking and hitting and grabbing at one another. Who shrieked nonsense syllables on command of cheerleaders without the slightest concept of either cheer or leadership. Who obeyed without question the guttural growls of the goose-stepping parodies of pride who double-marched them to doom.

The parade was endless.

But he could end it.

For a fleeting moment he sensed some symbolic similarity about all those he evoked; every one was, in a way, an authority figure. If so, it merely intensified his impulse.

He thought about it as he reached into the glove compartment for a handful of tissues and carefully wiped the dashboard instruments, the steering wheel, the rearview mirror. Bundling his discarded clothing in the wrappings which had enclosed the new, he placed the package under his arm and climbed

170

out. Again he used the tissues to wipe the door handles.

Peering through the shrubbery at the street beyond, he waited for a moment when no traffic was in sight, then stepped out onto the walk and started off. When he reached the intersection, he turned and made his way along a side street. Halfway up the block, he paused before one of a row of garbage cans, set out for emptying. Again he glanced around, making sure there was no traffic, no one to observe him. Then he lifted the lid of a container and dumped the wrapped clothing-bundle into the can, covering it with old newspapers. A grubby task, but the end justifies the means, however menial.

Turning away, he started down the street. There'd be a coffee shop somewhere near the intersection ahead. After he'd eaten, he must find another car—prowl the alleys behind the shops where the clerks and storekeepers parked, until he located a vehicle whose careless owner had left a key in the ignition. Another degrading exercise, but again he had to consider the end. The end he would bring to others.

What was that irritating inanity the hippies had leeched onto for their own? *Life-style.* A pretentious phrase for a filthy, irresponsible, empty existence with no style at all.

171

He was different. His life-style was death.
Thou shalt not kill.

God's commandment. But no one really heeded it, or heeded Him. Not with the mess the world was in. If God were running for reelection on his record, he'd lose.

Killing was easy. Everyone knows that. The hand swats the fly, the foot squashes the bug.

With some people, it stops there. But others go on. The farm wife, wringing the neck of the chicken. The stockyard workers in the slaughterhouse, clubbing the steer, butchering the squealing pigs.

The next step, of course, was war. But he didn't want to think about that. The massacre of the innocents.

Better to think about the righteous extermination of the guilty. It was a play, after all—a morality play, a passion play.

Passion. The worm stirred, gnawing his groin.

Suddenly, for no reason, he remembered the high school biology class and the dissection of a frog. He could see the bleached white underside of the creature, legs outstretched, as it wriggled on the table under the impalement of a knife.

And then the table became a bed, and the frog turned into a Prince—no, a Princess. A girl with bleached white skin, legs outstretched, wriggling under another impalement.

He knew who the girl was, of course.

And he'd be seeing her, today.

CHAPTER 17

When Karen finished dressing and came out into the living room, she was surprised to find Tom Doyle sitting there.

"I thought I wouldn't be seeing you again until this afternoon," she said.

"Somebody fouled up on the assignments downtown." Doyle shook his head. "The relief man never showed. They called and asked me to switch shifts, so I came along and took over from Lubeck."

"He left?"

"About an hour ago. You were still asleep. No sense disturbing you. I figured you needed the rest."

Karen nodded. She started towards the kitchen. "How about something to eat?"

"I could use a cup of coffee."

"Coming up."

Karen set the pot on, then fried herself an egg, put two slices of bread in the toaster, and took the orange juice from the refrigerator. The routine was automatic and somehow reassuring. Setting the table she could almost convince herself that this was just another day.

Doyle watched her from the kitchen doorway. "You look better this morning."

"I feel better." And she did. After that first nightmare Karen remembered nothing. She'd really slept.

The coffee was perking. Karen filled two cups, brought out the milk, turned the egg, deposited it on a plate just as the toast popped up. The choreography of habit, everything timed out perfectly. She carried her food to the table as Doyle took his place across from her.

The taste of toast and juice was reassuring, and so was the sight of the morning sun filter-

ing through the blinds. Then she remembered
something and started to rise from her chair.

Doyle glanced up. "Forget something?"

"The paper. They leave it outside the door."

"I brought it in."

"Where is it?"

"Please, Mrs. Raymond—sit down." Doyle
shifted uncomfortably in his chair. "Before
you look, maybe we'd better have a talk about
last night."

Karen sank back into her seat. "What happened?"

She reached for the coffee cup, but she didn't
drink. Because Doyle told her. Told her gently,
as if somehow the tone of his voice could
lessen the weight of the words. Jack Lorch,
Edna Drexel, Tony Rodell. Three of them; three
more gone, while she slept.

"Oh, my God," she said. "What are you
going to do?"

"Everything possible. The Sheriff's Department and the state police are working with
us." Doyle hesitated. "If there was only some
way to reach your husband—"

"I tell you I don't know where he is!" Karen
could scarcely hear the sound of her own voice
because of the pounding in her temples. "Don't
you think I want to find him, don't you think
I'm sick with worrying over this?" She stood

177

up. "I'm not the police—what do you expect from me?"

"Only your cooperation." For a moment Tom Doyle's voice held a hint of hostility. Then he shook his head unhappily. "We're trying our best, but there's so little to go on—"

"I know." Karen subsided. And something inside her said, *maybe you'd better tell him.*

Doyle was watching her. "Are you all right?"

"Of course." *On the other hand, what good would it do if he knew? Anything she said would only harm Bruce, and she couldn't do that. No matter what happened, she couldn't.*

"Look," said Doyle. "You don't have to go to work today. After what happened last night, you might be better off going downtown. You'd have a police matron assigned to you, but they wouldn't put you in a cell. It's just a matter of security—"

Karen shook her head. "I told my boss at the agency I was coming in. That's what I intend to do."

And she did, sitting silently beside Doyle in his car as he crawled through the congestion of the freeway, sun-visor shielding him from the glare.

While Doyle phoned in to report before leaving, Karen had managed to glance at the newspaper—just the headline and part of the lead story, but that was enough. Worse than the Tate-La Bianca murders, worse than anything. No wonder there was panic. And yet—

And yet these people on the freeway were streaming into the city. She glanced at the occupants of the cars around her. An elderly man in a shiny new Olds, his radio turned low to an early market report. A young mother in a compact crowded with kids, obviously aiming toward the delights of Disneyland. A fat matron in a white station wagon, probably on her way to a beauty salon, but twenty years too late. A handsome black youth driving an open Triumph, its dashboard speaker blasting the morning mouthings of Funny Freddy and the Top Forty.

Business as usual. Pleasure as usual. Even bumper-to-bumper, life went on. A man's skull shattered in a spatter of blood and whiskey, but Dow-Jones still computed the averages. A woman shrieked soundlessly under water and kiddies headed for the Submarine Ride and the delicious, make-believe perils of the Haunted House. A young man was ripped to pieces by snarling dogs, his body torn, his hands shredded, and an old woman wondered how much she'd tip her manicurist. And the screams and the groans and the snarls were all drowned out by the happy voice of Funny Freddy. Maybe these people carried fear inside them, fear

179

that whimpered and warned, but they twisted the dial and listened to the Top Forty instead.

What else could they do? And what else could she do with the fear she felt? Go to work, that's all. Pretend, like all the others, that this was just another day and that the night would never come.

They turned onto the Harbor Freeway and took one of the ramps leading off into the mercantile maze of the downtown area.

"This your building?" Doyle asked, and she nodded. He eased the car over to the curb. A policeman's lot is not a happy one, but at least he doesn't have to worry about finding a parking place.

Riding up in the elevator with Doyle, she had a bad moment. There was a contraction of the stomach muscles which had nothing to do with the soaring motion of ascent. *Gut feeling.* Another one of those stupid catch-phrases she detested, because its indiscriminate use deadened all meaning, but she understood the original concept now. There was a ball in her stomach, a cold hard ball coiling around her intestines, a ball of fear. Not the fear of turning her back on an unseen killer, but the fear of facing the people she knew. The people who knew her, and who must know, now, about Bruce.

Doyle was watching her. "Nervous?" he murmured.

Karen ran her tongue over dry lips, shaking her head quickly. She wished he'd stop watching her, stop asking if she was all right. On the other hand, she acknowledged, it was his job.

And this was hers.

Stepping out of the elevator, she led Doyle to the door of the reception room. He opened it, allowing her to move past him.

Peggy's head bobbed up from behind the glass fronting the reception desk.

"Oh—good morning." There was something not quite right about her voice, and something definitely wrong with her hasty smile as she stared past Karen at Tom Doyle.

Karen nodded towards him as she spoke. "This is Mr. Doyle. He's with—"

"Yes, I know." Peggy broke in hastily. "They called and told Mr. Haskane there'd be somebody with you. I'll let him know you're here."

"That won't be necessary," Karen began, but Peggy turned away and plugged in the switchboard.

Why, she's more embarrassed than I am! The realization came to Karen, and when the corridor door opened and Ed Haskane emerged, it was obvious that he was embarrassed, too.

"Good to see you," he said, acknowledging

her presence and Doyle's introduction with a gesture as inept and uncharacteristic as his phrase. "Of course, you didn't have to come in today, I told you on the phone—"

"I wanted to come in," Karen said. She was all right now, no more gut feeling. "No sense letting the work pile up."

"Right." Haskane glanced at Doyle as Karen started into the corridor. "I, uh, suppose you'll be coming in, too?"

Doyle nodded and followed Karen. The trio advanced down the hall, past the oak-doored offices, past Media, Art and Copy. Karen had a feeling that these doors were opening and closing in a faster tempo than was usual, but she couldn't be sure. If others eyed their progress, it was with silent discretion, and it didn't bother her. After all, what was there for anyone to see? She didn't have two heads. Perhaps they were looking at her merely to assure themselves that she still retained one.

To take her mind off the matter, she started talking before they turned into the second corridor.

"What happened with Girnbach? Did they okay the copy?"

"Oh, that—" Haskane smiled quickly. "They thought your stuff was great. But they didn't go for the artwork. I've put Frisby on it, he's noodled out something new. Of course that means we'll have to do a little rewrite, more in line with the drawing—"

The same old story. Business as usual. Karen recalled how often she'd bitched to herself about this kind of nonsense, but right now she welcomed it. Give her something to occupy her mind.

"You want to send it down?" she asked.

"Sure, if you feel up to taking another swing."

"I'm ready." Karen moved through the open doorway of her cubicle. Doyle entered behind her as Ed Haskane hesitated in the hall.

"Okay," he said. "I'll shoot it over. But if you don't—I mean, if there's anything I can do—"

"Don't worry, Mr. Haskane," Karen said. "I'm all right, thank you."

Haskane disappeared.

She knew what he meant; what he really wanted to do was talk to her about what had happened. About how it feels to have a husband in the sanatorium and go walking in there to find—

But he wouldn't ask outright. He wouldn't, because she wasn't giving him a chance.

Karen turned and shed her jacket. The detective stood behind her, an awkward intrusion in these cramped confines.

"Why don't you sit down over there?" Karen

indicated a chair. "Take your coat off if you like."

"This is fine." Doyle sat down.

"You'll find some magazines in the top drawer of the file. Mostly fashion stuff, I'm afraid, but at least it's something to read."

"Thanks."

But Doyle didn't read any magazines. And when the runner brought in the rough for the artwork with her old copy clipped to the top, he watched Karen work.

He was quiet, and out of her range of vision, but the mere knowledge of his presence threw Karen off a bit. Or was it knowing the *reason* for his presence that bothered her?

In either case, she had a bad morning. The new rough was done in a totally different style, and the motorcycle had been eliminated. This meant the heading had to be changed. And once that went, the copy inevitably went with it.

She made three or four futile attempts and filled her wastebasket with wadded paper until the contents resembled a pile of popcorn balls. Finally, around noon, she got what she wanted.

She called Haskane.

"Good," he said. "Look, I've got a twelve-thirty lunch. Suppose we go over it when I get back."

"What did you say?"

His voice was faint. "How about two-thirty in my office?"

"Two-thirty?"

"That's right. See you."

Karen hung up and turned to Doyle. "The phone," she said. "It's bugged, isn't it?"

Doyle shrugged. "Matter of precaution."

Karen made no comment. Instead she reached for her jacket.

"Where to now?" Doyle asked.

"It's lunch time." Karen opened her purse, inspected herself in the compact mirror. "I suppose we eat together."

"Sorry." Doyle smiled apologetically.

"I know." Karen put her compact away. "Matter of precaution."

In the outer corridor before the elevator, a ruddy-faced man with a ginger mustache leaned against the wall, folding the classified section of a newspaper. He paid no attention to them until Doyle nodded.

"We're going to lunch," he said.

The man looked up. "How long?"

Doyle's eyes questioned Karen.

"Forty-five minutes. There's a grill downstairs."

The man glanced at his watch. "I'll be here," he told Doyle.

In the descending elevator the lanky detective cleared his throat. "No sense playing games. The way I figure, you're better off knowing we meant what we said about security. Your receptionist's tipped off—if anyone she doesn't recognize shows up and wants to get into the office, she'll check with the man on duty outside before admitting him."

"I suppose you've got somebody in the grill, too?"

"That wouldn't be necessary, not in a public place."

"Good." Karen smiled. "Then it doesn't matter if we go somewhere else."

"What's wrong with the grill?"

"Too many people from the office eating there. I think I'd feel more comfortable down the block. It's only a cafeteria, but there won't be anyone staring at me."

"Whatever you like."

Karen picked up a salad, iced tea and a scoop of lemon sherbet. But when she and Doyle found a table, she barely touched her food.

"I thought you were hungry," Doyle said.

"I was. Until I saw that." Karen indicated the table directly to her right where a pudgy man in a seersucker jacket sat reading an early edition of the afternoon paper. The bold headline was plainly visible: DRUGGED DOGS KILL THIRD ASYLUM ESCAPEE.

"Is it true?" Karen murmured.

"Yes. They got the lab reports."

"How awful." Karen's hand curled around the side of the iced-tea glass. "Tony Rodell. I think I've heard some of his records. I never knew he was in that sanatorium, too."

"Your husband didn't mention him?"

"I told you, I didn't see Bruce while he was there."

"That's right, I forgot." Doyle took a bite of his ham sandwich.

Karen relinquished her grasp on the glass, but the chill remained. "I keep thinking about that boy. What kind of a person would do such a thing to him?"

Doyle munched, swallowed. "Depends."

"I know it's a silly question." Karen nodded. "All sorts of people commit murder—I suppose you've seen a lot of them."

"A few." Doyle used his napkin, put it down on the table. "No, I take that back, I've probably seen plenty. And so have you."

"What do you mean?"

"According to statistics, less than half the homicides in this country result in an arrest. And only a small percentage of those arrested are actually convicted and sentenced."

"But we read all these articles about scientific crime investigation—"

"Sure you do. And we've got lab men, technicians, all kinds of fancy equipment. Sometimes it works. And when it does, everybody takes a bow." Doyle's smile was grim. "But I'll give it to you straight. Over ninety percent of all homicides that are solved, the culprit is handed to the department on a silver platter."

"What do you mean?"

"Either he walks in and gives himself up, or somebody fingers him."

"An informer?"

Doyle nodded. "That's when the real police work usually begins—gathering evidence for a conviction. But first you've got to make an arrest. And nine times out of ten that comes about because somebody tips us off." Doyle was watching her. "I'm not talking about a professional informer or even an eyewitness. Most of the time it's somebody close—a friend, a member of the family who knows, or suspects. At first they're usually inclined to button up, but after a while, when they have a chance to think it over, they realize they've got to speak out. It's their duty to prevent such a thing from happening again, if you follow me."

"I follow you." Karen stared at him. "Right up to the line. But I'm not stepping over. If you expect me to say yes, Bruce is guilty, just forget it. Not because he's my husband, but because I don't know. Do you understand that? I don't know!"

"Mrs. Raymond—"

Karen stood up. "It's time to get back to the office," she said.

And that was the last thing she said to him until they were back in her little cubicle on the tenth floor. There she picked up the rough and her copy and started for the hall.

"It's time for me to see my boss," she told him. "His office is around the corner in the other corridor."

"I'll walk you over."

"Suit yourself." She picked up the phone and notified Haskane that she was on her way.

Doyle followed her in silence to the door of Haskane's office. "Go ahead," he said. "I'll wait outside here." He opened the door for her. "Look, I'm sorry I sounded off like that. I didn't mean—"

"I know what you meant." Karen moved past him and shut the door behind her.

Ed Haskane was at his desk. He looked up and started to open his mouth, but Karen beat him to the punch.

"I'm still all right," she said, spreading the rough and the attached typewritten sheet on the desk top before him. "And I think the copy is, too."

Whatever his hang-ups, Haskane had a life-long love affair with language; it was his se-mantic interest that had made him a copy chief. The sight of the typed or printed word was enough to set his juices flowing, and she sensed the salivation as he turned his atten-tion to what she was presenting.

"Uh huh—yes—I think this does it." He looked up, rubbing his cheek. "Just one thing, your heading. The kids will get it, but what does *A Wipe-Out* mean to the straight au-dience?"

"I hadn't thought about it that way." Karen frowned.

"Well, maybe you can tie it in somewhere after the lead paragraph." Haskane stood up. "Excuse me a minute, will you? As we say in Mexico, I have to use the Juan."

He disappeared into the private washroom and closed the door.

It was warm in the office, despite the air-conditioning, but Karen felt a sudden resur-gence of the chill that had assailed her when she'd learned how Tony Rodell died. *A Wipe-Out.* Just a hype phrase, hyperbole to the teen-agers. But Haskane was right. To an older, straighter generation there was another mean-ing. And it was *that* meaning which had un-consciously urged the phrase upon her when she wrote the copy this morning. Wipe out. Destroy. Annihilate. Kill.

A signal button blinked from the base of Haskane's phone. She picked up the receiver automatically and habit modulated her voice. "Mr. Haskane's office."

"Karen."

She didn't say anything. She couldn't.

"Karen—do you know who this is?"

"Yes."

"I asked for your extension, but they switched me here. Are you alone?"

"For the moment."

"Then listen. What time is your afternoon coffee-break?"

"Four o'clock."

"Good. I'll be waiting for you. Upstairs, on the roof."

"I—I don't know if I can get away—"

"You must. I've got to talk to you. This may be the only chance."

Karen heard the muffled flushing sound from behind the door beyond.

"Where are you?" Karen murmured.

"Four o'clock on the roof," the voice whispered.

And then it was gone.

CHAPTER 18

When Karen left Haskane's office, she found Doyle waiting outside in the hall where she'd left him.

"Everything all right?" he asked.

Karen was sick of the question; she'd heard it so often during the past two days; it was as meaningless as the show of solicitude behind it. Nobody really wanted to hear an answer, any more than they did when they asked, "How are you?" Doyle, of all people, certainly knew that everything was far from being right with her, and he didn't really care. He was just on an assignment and merely wanted assurance there'd be no immediate problems with his charge.

She wanted to tell him that things could hardly be worse. But her present purposes didn't allow for arousing his uneasiness or suspicion.

So Karen nodded, and they walked back around the corner to the cubicle.

"Use your phone?" Doyle asked.

"Help yourself."

Doyle called in to report while Karen arranged the rough layout and copy on her desk beside the typewriter. She made a show of concentration, but didn't miss a word of Doyle's murmurings. Everything was under control, and yes, he'd expect Gordon at five o'clock.

Gordon would be Doyle's relief man, Karen decided; he'd take over the next shift. But five o'clock—that meant Doyle would still be on duty here with her when she went to the roof.

If she went to the roof . . .

Doyle finished his call and hung up.

"Any news?" she asked.

He shook his head. "They located Rodell's car. If there's anything else, the department's not releasing it yet."

194

"No word about my husband?"

"Sorry. They didn't say."

Karen turned away. No news is good news. Or was it?

If she went to the roof . . .

Almost three o'clock now. She had just about an hour to decide.

"I've got to rewrite some copy," she told Doyle.

"Go ahead." Doyle opened the file, selected a magazine at random, grimaced at the emaciated model on the cover whose dazed expression lent a double meaning to the term "high fashion."

Karen sat down before her typewriter and reached for paper.

The problem was how to handle *A Wipe-Out.* She solved it in a little under twenty minutes by injecting two equally meaningless tie-in phrases under the first paragraph of her copyblock. Then she retyped slowly, concentrating on the real problem.

The roof . . .

She couldn't hold out forever, she knew that. Maybe the sensible thing would be to tell Doyle now, get it over with. Let the police handle everything; after all, it was their job. Nobody had hired her to take risks in the line of duty. Unless being married in itself entailed duty.

Not according to Women's Lib. A woman's

first duty was to herself; marriage in its present form was as obsolete as the concept of original sin.

But not for Karen. Intellectually, she realized the necessity of emancipation; emotionally, she was unable to break free from her commitment. So that was no problem, really. Because there was no choice. She had to go because she had to find out the truth, once and for all. Even if it meant finding out the truth about herself, learning that she'd been wrong.

Of course, if she was wrong, the knowledge would come too late. But it wouldn't matter then.

All that mattered now was getting to the roof.

Karen glanced at her watch. Quarter to four. Doyle was leafing through another fashion magazine, scowling at the latest inspiration of genius offered by Yves St. Laurent. Left to himself, he'd sit here until his relief arrived at five o'clock. But the question was how to leave him to himself. Suddenly she had the answer.

Karen pushed her chair back, stood up.

Doyle lowered the magazine. "Where are we going now?"

She reached for her purse. "I don't know about you, but there's a powder room down the hall."

"Oh, sure." He was smiling now. "I'll escort you."

"As far as the door." Karen returned his smile. "This is a very proper agency."

Ten minutes of four.

The coffee break hadn't started, and the corridor was deserted. The employees' washrooms were just around the corner, at right angles to the passage leading back to the entrance. Karen paused before the door marked *Ladies*, glancing at Tom Doyle as she gripped her purse.

"I'll probably be a while," she said. "I want to put on fresh makeup before we go for coffee."

"Take your time."

Karen entered the washroom. She didn't put on makeup and she didn't take her time. The moment she assured herself that the place was deserted, she walked straight through— and out on the other side. What Doyle didn't realize was that there was another door which fronted on the hall outside the offices.

Emerging from it, she found herself in an outer corridor around the corner from the elevators. That was good, because the man on duty there couldn't see her. All she had to do was continue walking in the opposite direction to the heavy metal door under the *Exit* sign.

She opened it and saw the stairs. Moving slowly to avoid the clatter of her heels on the iron treads, she started up. After two flights she could feel the perspiration on her forehead, but her mouth was dry. Her breathing quickened, though not from exertion.

Five minutes to four.

Five minutes to four, and she was on the roof.

Alone.

It wasn't the first time Karen had made the climb; long ago, when she started at the agency, some of the girls had been in the habit of bringing their lunches and eating them here while acquiring a suntan. But she'd never come up by herself, and since an office memo had gone the rounds to forbid the practice, the roof had been off-limits. Not hard to understand why. Aside from the projection of the skylight at the stairtop, the roof was perfectly flat, and there was no wall, no railing to separate the level limits of the edge from the emptiness beyond. A high wind would constitute a definite danger.

But there was no wind today, only the burning heat. The roof's surface was gritty underfoot. The afternoon sun was slanting towards Santa Monica in the west, and Karen turned her back to it, moving slowly to survey the shaded sectors of the city.

Strange, she realized. *This is the only time I ever see them.* Off to the north stretched La

Crescenta, La Canada, Altadena—exotic names for sunbaked suburbs hidden in the hills. She'd never been to any of them. Somewhat closer, rising out of the smog of Glendale, was Forest Lawn.

Karen turned her back to the scene, gazing at Boyle Heights and East Los Angeles beyond, then south towards Watts. Again these were merely names to her; names associated with poverty and protest. Not nice places to live, though most of the city's population was concentrated here. Those who could choose lived west of the downtown area; when they talked about Los Angeles they were really speaking of Hollywood, Beverly Hills, Bel Air, Brentwood, even Malibu. If they had to drive through to the east and south, they took a freeway, racing past the realities to some make-believe destination: Knott's Berry Farm, the Japanese Gardens. But all the while a million people sweltered and suffered in the sun-bleached slums.

No wonder there was hatred and hostility here, the omnipresent threat of riot. They talked about the climate of violence and debated its components; some said it was the war and others blamed war toys; some accused the political far right, others the political far left. But here on the roof the real climate of violence was plainly apparent; it was a climate of humid heat and sour smells enveloping the ghetto areas.

Four o'clock.

Karen turned back towards the skylight.

The roof was still empty. Empty and still.

What had happened?

Why didn't he come?

She squinted into the sun and perspiration rivuleted against the corners of her eyes. Hot. Too hot. The climate of violence—

She had to turn away. A cloud slid over the sun, and a tiny breeze sprang up. Gratefully she moved against it, towards the east edge of the roof.

Glancing down at the street, she saw the traffic crawling like windup toys fourteen flights below. As she stared over the edge she felt a surge of giddiness and took a single step backwards.

Suddenly the breeze grew stronger. She started to turn.

And the hand gripped her arm.

CHAPTER 19

The stranger was tall, his broad shoulders cramped in a jacket that was a size too small for him. His skin was very white. Pale as a ghost, because he was a ghost.

"Bruce!"

Karen stared at him, hoping that uttering the name would make the stranger disappear, leave only the man she remembered. But six months is a long time and he wasn't the same.

"Did anyone see you come up here?" he murmured.

"No."

"You're positive?"

Karen nodded. "Lucky thing you reached me on Haskane's line. My phone is bugged. And I've got a detective bodyguard."

"Where is he?"

Quickly, Karen explained how she'd eluded Doyle. As she did so, Bruce's fixed frown relaxed, and so did his grip on her arm. "Then we can talk."

"Why didn't you get in touch with me before? I've been going out of my mind—"

Karen broke off, realizing the import of the phrase. But Bruce merely shook his head, expression unchanged.

"I figured they'd be monitoring the calls at the apartment."

"But where have you been? What happened?"

"No time for that now." Bruce's frown returned. "If they realize you cut out on them and start looking for you—"

"What if they do?" Karen tried to keep her voice steady. "You can't go on running forever."

"I have to." Bruce's eyes never left her face. "They already know I was in the sanatorium. They're bound to check my service record and the hospital reports. Between that and what we both know about me—" He broke off and for a moment his glance wavered. Then he stared at her again, and his words came with a rush. "Have you said anything? Have you told them about us?"

Karen shook her head.

"Good." Bruce's shoulders sagged in relief. "That's what I had to find out. Because if they knew, that would be the clincher, wouldn't it?"

"Is this the reason you wanted to see me?"

"You don't understand, do you?" Bruce turned away, but his murmur was all too audible. "You don't know what it means. To sit there, day after day. Night after night. After a while, the two seem to blend. Not blend, really, because it's as if the night swallowed the day. So you're always in darkness, perpetual darkness—a night-world. That's what you live in, a night-world, where all the sounds and shadows turn strange. And you think about those who've done this to you, and they're your enemies. Then you think about those who aren't directly responsible, but who don't care. The people you call out to who never hear your voice—after a while you realize they're your enemies, too. Everyone's a part of the conspiracy, a conspiracy of silence and indifference. They're all trying to get you. So you wonder how you can get them first. Punish them for punishing you. And you start to dream about it, and the dream becomes a plan and the plan becomes a reality."

"Bruce, for God's sake—"

"We don't talk about God in the asylum. We talk about something called the Id and the Ego and the Superego. Father, Son and the Holy Ghost, all equally invisible." His smile was bitter. "The gospel according to Griswold. According to him there are no accidents. The mind that makes one man a murderer makes another man a victim."

"Is that what you believe?"

"Of course not." Bruce sighed. "I'm only trying to tell you what it's like, tell you how he thinks. I know, because that's how I felt myself, at first. But Griswold helped me change. The thing is, he couldn't help *him*."

"Who?"

"The man they're looking for. The murderer."

"What's his name?"

Bruce shook his head. "If you knew his name, he'd come after you. Do you want to be a victim, too?"

"I want to help you."

"Then give me some money—let me get away before he finds me. That's all I want."

"Is it?"

"No." And then he was holding her, his arms tight, his body close so that she could feel the trembling. "You're what I want, what I've always wanted, I know that now. But it's

204

too late, after what happened I don't blame you—"

"I love you. I always have."

The trembling ceased. Now there was only a tautness. "You didn't even visit me out there."

"Griswold asked me not to. He must have told you that."

"Yes. And I didn't believe him."

"I was coming to see you the other night. Griswold said you were probably ready to come home."

"If I'd only known." Bruce released her, stepped back.

"You didn't?"

"Do you think I'd have gone along with Cromer if I had?"

"Cromer—?"

"All right." Bruce took a deep breath. "The man they want is Edmund Cromer. He never really talked about himself, but from what little I heard, he's the only son of a wealthy family back in New York or New Jersey, I'm not sure which. They committed him about a year ago. In view of what's happened, I suspect they sent him all the way out here because he might have been involved in something pretty horrible back East."

"Did you know about his plan to escape?"

"Nobody did, except Rodell. And I don't

think Rodell realized he meant to kill anyone when he made the break. But of course Cromer must have had it all worked out. And after it started, there was no stopping."

"How did it happen?"

"I'm not sure. I was upstairs in my room after dinner, and so were the others, all but Cromer. He'd gone down to talk to Dr. Griswold. He must have killed him first, in the electrotherapy room, then the night nurse outside. There was no noise. The first time any of us realized something had happened was when we smelled smoke from the burning papers in the fireplace."

"Wasn't there an attendant on duty with you upstairs?"

"That's right—Thomas. He was playing checkers with Tony Rodell in his room. I guess that had all been arranged, just to keep him busy, because Cromer had no trouble finding him when he came in with the knife in his hand—"

Bruce broke off, frowning. "No point going into that," he said. "Thomas was dead by the time the rest of us came running out of our rooms. The old lady, Mrs. Freeling, took one look at Thomas and keeled over. Cromer said she was dead."

"You didn't examine her?"

"No." Bruce shook his head quickly. "And

I didn't try to stop Cromer either, if that's what you're wondering about. None of us did. Because Cromer had come upstairs carrying Dr. Griswold's gun and he kept us covered. We had no way of knowing it wasn't loaded—all we did know was that Cromer had committed cold-blooded murder and was perfectly capable of continuing.

"He gave us our choice. Go with him now in Griswold's car or he'd leave us behind. And he didn't say anything about leaving us behind alive.

"If we'd had time to think, maybe a couple of us could have gotten together and tried to jump him. But you've got to realize what it was like—the panic, the confusion. Edna Drexel was hysterical, Lorch was in a state of shock. Between Rodell and Cromer with his gun, I had no chance of doing anything alone. I guess all any of us could grasp was that we'd better get out of there.

"Cromer promised to take us into town. Before we drove off he gave Rodell the gun and told him to use it if anyone made a move. Then he took the freeway to Sherman Oaks. He left the car, saying he'd be back in a few minutes, and Rodell stayed behind with the gun. That's when I made my move. I got it away from him, but while we were struggling, the others ran off. After Tony was knocked out, I found the gun was empty, but I had no way of knowing where Cromer had gone, or if he'd really come back. And perhaps, if he did, he'd have another weapon. What I wanted to do, of course, was drive off—but Cromer had taken the car keys." Bruce's voice dropped to a whisper. "So I ran."

"I understand." Karen put her hand on his arm. "But you don't have to run anymore."

Bruce's smile was bleak. "Meaning you believe me?"

"Of course I do—"

"You're not the police."

"Bruce, you've got to talk to them. If you'd tell them what you told me—"

"What good would it do? I'm their number one suspect. They aren't going to take my word for anything unless I can come up with some proof."

"Then cooperate with them, help the police find this man Cromer. You know what he looks like, you can give them a description."

"Sure I can." Bruce shrugged. "But that doesn't mean they'll believe me." He stared at Karen, and the bleak smile turned grim. "Maybe there is no Edmund Cromer. Maybe I made the whole thing up."

"But you didn't! I know—and I can prove it."

"How?"

Quickly, Karen described her experience in the apartment and how she'd discovered the attempt to force open the bathroom window.

Bruce's eyes narrowed. "They don't know about this?"

"I didn't want them to know. But I can tell them now. And I can show them the marks, where he tried to pry his way in."

"They could say it was coincidence. Or that you made those marks yourself."

"You and I know better than that." Karen's fingers tightened involuntarily on her husband's arm. "Don't you see? Somebody was trying to get at me. And he's still on the loose. What if he decides to try again? I'll never be safe unless you help—"

Bruce hesitated, but only for a moment. "All right. What do you want me to do?"

"This detective who's guarding me—Tom Doyle. You've got to talk to him."

"What about his partner, the one you said is in the hall outside the office?"

"He doesn't know anything about this, neither of them do. They don't even know I left."

"So what do you suppose will happen if he sees you show up from nowhere with some stranger?" Bruce shook his head. "The way things are now, they're all trigger-happy. I'm not taking that kind of chance."

"I don't know the man outside, but Doyle isn't like that. You can trust him."

"Then let him trust me." Bruce's voice was strained. "If you want me to talk to Doyle, tell him to come here. And tell him to come alone."

CHAPTER 20

"Trust him?" Doyle said. "After the trick you just pulled on me? I don't trust either one of you."

Karen faced the detective in the corridor outside the washroom. "I'm sorry. It's the only way."

"No, it isn't. I'm putting in a call right now. In five minutes we'll have this building surrounded. If anybody goes up to that roof, there'll be a full squad backstopping him. No more risks."

"What about the risk to Bruce?" Karen fought to keep her voice steady. "Can't you understand what he's been through these past two days? He's been sick, you know that. There's no telling what he'll do if he thinks he's been betrayed. I gave him my word."

"I know," Doyle murmured. "But you said it yourself. There's no telling what he might do under pressure."

"There won't be any pressure, not if you go alone. I did and he didn't harm me. He hasn't any weapons." Karen's words came quickly. "Look, he's the only one who can tell you what really happened. He was there, he saw it. He wants to help. But you've got to give him a chance."

Doyle took her arm. "Come with me."

He led her along the hall, around the corner to the elevator bank. The man with the ginger mustache was still leaning against the wall, his newspaper tucked underneath his arm. Doyle moved towards him.

"Okay, Harry," he said.

The man looked up.

"Harry, this is Mrs. Raymond. Mrs. Raymond, Harry Forbes." Doyle didn't wait for either of them to acknowledge the introduction. "Now listen to me. Something's come up—"

Forbes listened, nodding several times.

"Right," he said. "You're going to the roof. I take Mrs. Raymond back to her office and keep an eye on her there." He hesitated. "What do we do about holding the fort out in front here?"

"On your way in tell the girl at the reception desk she's to admit nobody—and I mean just that, nobody at all, under any circumstances—until I give her the word. Anybody shows up, they'll have to wait. Oh, and one thing more."

Doyle left Karen's side and approached Forbes, his voice sinking to a murmur. Again Forbes nodded. "Got it." He walked over to Karen. "Come with me, please."

Karen turned to glance at Doyle, but he was already punching the UP button beside the elevators. "Please," she called. "Remember what I told you. He's very upset—"

"Don't worry."

Karen caught the profile of his smile as the elevator door opened. He stepped into the car.

"Let's go." Forbes was holding the office door for her. As soon as she entered, he moved past her to Peggy at the reception desk. Showing his badge, he repeated Doyle's instructions. Peggy nodded, then glanced up over his shoulder towards Karen. She looked as if she were going to say something, but Forbes didn't give her a chance; taking Karen's arm, he led her to the door of the corridor.

Once inside, he hastened with her down the hall.

"What's your hurry?" Karen said.

"Got to place a call."

And when they reached her cubicle around the corner, he did.

Listening, Karen felt numb realization. *He lied. He doublecrossed me.*

But Doyle hadn't lied, because he hadn't made her any promises. And it wasn't a double-cross, just a compromise. He'd gone to the roof alone, the way she'd told him. But he'd also given Forbes instructions to phone for a squad. *No more risks.* But if so, why hadn't he waited until the squad arrived? The answer was self-apparent; he wanted to make sure Bruce didn't have time to get away.

Forbes turned to her now, phone in hand. "Mrs. Raymond?"

"Yes—"

"I want you to give me a description of your husband. Physical appearance, what he's wearing."

Of course. Just in case he *did* try to get away. Karen's first angry impulse was to tell him to go to hell, but what good would it do? Doyle would be bringing Bruce down, anyway. Besides, she had already given a description to Sergeant Cole at the sanatorium.

So she told Forbes what he wanted to know, and he repeated it, phrase for phrase, into the mouthpiece of the phone.

"Height, six-two. Weight, one-eighty. Eyes, gray. Complexion, fair. Blue jacket, gray trousers. Blue and white striped shirt, no necktie—"

This is the way it ends, Karen thought. *No bang, not even a whimper. They pick him up, they question him and then—*

And then what?

She'd told Bruce they'd believe him, that his statement would help them track down the murderer. But suppose they were already convinced he was guilty?

There was no answer. If Bruce was innocent, and the police thought otherwise, then she'd betrayed him. And if he really was guilty, her advice was still a betrayal. Either way, she told herself, nothing could be worse.

But she was wrong.

What happened next came very quickly.

Forbes finished his conversation on the phone. He started to turn to Karen, then glanced up past her. Karen followed his gaze to the open doorway.

There was a sudden echo of sound along the hall in the distance; an excited murmuring, the quick clatter of hurrying footsteps.

And now Ed Haskane appeared, eyes wide, mouth moving.

Forbes stared at him. "What is it?"

"You'd better come—"

"Where?"

But Haskane had already turned and started to stumble off.

Forbes rose, beckoning to Karen. Together, they moved into the hall. Haskane had already rounded the corner of the corridor when they caught up with him.

"Tell me what happened," the detective said.

"I'll show you." Haskane's reply was almost lost in the confusion of sound from beyond the far end of the hall.

"Where?"

"The window—"

The window was in the outer office, on the far wall behind Peggy's reception desk. It was open, and Peggy stood before it in an excited group of agency employees. All of them were staring down, and when Forbes forced his way through, he and Karen stared down, too.

There was a body lying in the street below.

CHAPTER 21

For a moment Karen's vision blurred. She started to sway; then felt Forbes's grip on her arm.

"Let's go," he said.

"Down there? No—I can't—"

"You're coming with me."

She felt the pressure of his fingers as they turned and moved away from the window, and that was real. But leaving the office wasn't real, and the descent in the elevator was a floating with everything disoriented the way it must be in free fall.

Free fall. The body pitching from the rooftop, sprawling in the street. *Bruce*—

Traffic was halted, backed up with horns blaring. Crowds circled on the sidewalk, held against the curb by a hastily formed cordon of uniformed officers. Karen was dimly conscious of the sirens screaming in the distance, dully aware that police cars were squealing and screeching through an opening at the intersection beyond, followed by an ambulance. But none of this was real, either. The only reality was what lay spattered against the pavement, lay facedown like a broken doll, its limbs twisted at grotesque angles.

She didn't want to look at it, but she had to. Because it wasn't a doll. It was real, and she could see the familiar clothing, the hair, she recognized everything. Not a doll. And not Bruce.

"Doyle!" Forbes said. "Oh, Christ—!"

For a moment the surge of relief was so intense she wanted to cry out. Instead, she gasped.

The sound of her voice was lost in the clamor. People were jostling from the walk behind; someone buffeted her in the back, but Karen was only vaguely aware of the blow. A group of men crossed from a police car pulled up against the curb, and she saw that the man in the lead was Lieutenant Barringer.

Forbes saw him, too. "Wait here," he said. "I'll be right back."

There was no need for him to command her, because she had nowhere to go. Running away wouldn't help, after what had happened; nothing would help. All she could do was wait.

Karen watched while Forbes approached Lieutenant Barringer. She saw Barringer glance up as Forbes pointed in her direction; then, for a moment, her view was obscured by the ambulance attendants as they moved in with their stretcher.

She turned away, not wanting to see what happened when they bent over the crumpled corpse of Tom Doyle. But the people around her did not turn away, and she could hear their shocked murmurs.

Then Forbes was at her side again, taking her arm.

Karen frowned up at him. "Where are we going?"

"Lieutenant Barringer wants you to wait in the office. He's sending someone up to get your statement there. Sergeant Gordon, he said. He'll be looking out for you."

"What are they going to do?"

"Barringer didn't say. Gordon will have instructions when he sees you." Forbes shrugged.

"Right now we've got to clear the streets. One hell of a mess for a peak traffic hour."

One hell of a mess, but the main problem is to clear the street so all the Daddies won't be late for dinner. Karen shook her head. But Forbes was right, of course. The living are the ones to be considered; the dead have no problems.

"All right, break it up—there's nothing to see—let's move along now—." A cordon of officers moved along the curb, chanting their familiar formulas.

Forbes led Karen to the building entrance, and there were more police there, stationed on either side of the doorway, and halting people for identification and questioning as they attempted to exit. She noticed some of her own co-workers in the line beyond the door, waiting their turn for interrogation.

"We've got the garage downstairs covered, too," Forbes told her. "Nobody gets in or out without identification."

He displayed his own I.D. to one of the officers as they entered. "I'm taking Mrs. Raymond inside," he said. "Lieutenant Barringer's orders. Could you see to it that she gets up to her office? Sutherland Agency, tenth floor."

The officer nodded and turned to summon a uniformed man from the group examining employees from the building inside.

220

Karen glanced at Forbes. "You're not coming?"

"Barringer wants me to stay here." He released her arm. "Don't worry, you'll be in safe hands."

Karen nodded, then turned and followed her new escort to the elevators.

They ascended in silence. No one was entering the building and most of the offices would be emptying at this hour.

The Sutherland Agency was no exception. Peggy's desk was vacant, and the rooms lining the hall beyond were echoing and empty. Even the few who normally might have lingered to make last-minute calls or finish last-minute assignments had been lured downstairs by the earlier excitement.

Excitement? There was nothing exciting about death. It was the violence that drew them. She remembered what Bruce had just told her. Maybe we all have a night-world—

"Will you be all right, Mrs. Raymond?" the officer said.

There it was again, the same phrase. She summoned the automatic reply. "Of course."

He closed the door and left her alone in the office. And she didn't want to be alone anymore, not even for a moment. Why couldn't Forbes have come back to wait with her?

She knew the answer, of course. The reason

Barringer wanted him downstairs was to get his statement. Get it first, before she was questioned. So if there were any discrepancies, any lies, he'd be able to check back.

Not that lying would do any good now. It never had. If only she'd told the truth from the beginning—the whole truth—

Karen started down the hall towards her office, then hesitated. The hollow sound of her own footsteps halted her, and she stood there, conscious that she was trembling.

You're afraid.

All right, admit it. Everyone's afraid nowadays. Afraid of driving and getting smashed on the freeway, afraid of walking and being mugged in the street. Afraid of losing a job and starving, afraid of keeping a job and ending up on an insufficient pension which meant starving in old age. Afraid of the bomb and germ warfare and nerve gas and other manmade devices of destruction, afraid of the natural disasters of earthquake and fire and flood.

No wonder the younger generation turned on with grass and smack while their elders turned to barbiturates and alcohol and cigarettes. *I'll say one thing for cancer—it certainly takes your mind off your troubles.*

She remembered Bruce saying that, long ago. Before he went into the sanatorium, when he had this thing about death. He'd said a lot of things. *When a corpse goes to the morgue, they identify it by fastening a tag to the big toe. But where do they put the tag if the toes are missing? And what does it matter? A corpse has no identity. I've seen hundreds of them overseas, and they're all alike. What do the maggots care about name, rank and serial number?*

Bruce had this fear of death, and it was only to be expected, after what he'd been through.

But was it natural to be afraid of life?

Karen paced the floor behind the reception desk. She had no intention of going down the hall to her office now. There she'd be isolated. Here she could at least keep her eye on the door.

She moved to the window, noting that it was getting dark outside. Was she frightened of *that*, too?

No, the dark was harmless. What she dreaded were the people who prowled it. The citizens of the night-world. Karen shook her head. No point in losing perspective. The world, day or night, wasn't really all that bad.

She stared out across the city. Long ago, before she was born, Los Angeles had been looked upon as some sort of earthly paradise where there was sunshine every day and the stars glittered every night. Now that image had faded, tarnished by technology, and perhaps this was the reason so many mocked it. But was it actually any worse than New York or London, Moscow or Peking?

In spite of her earlier reflections on the rooftop, it was necessary to remember that millions of people lived out there, and most of them were very much like herself. Reasonably honest, decent, and trustworthy; trying to live up to their responsibilities to family, friends, the strictures of society.

So it was only the few she feared. And even then, she wasn't really alarmed as long as she could recognize them. Most of the creeps and weirdos—and she wasn't using terms of prejudice, she reminded herself; didn't they proudly proclaim themselves as freaks?—were easily spotted and could be easily avoided. They were no great menace as long as one steered clear of them and their haunts.

The danger came from the others. The ones you loved. The ones you surrendered yourself to because you wanted them, needed them.

There was no mystery about what she was afraid of. Deep down inside she knew there was only one real fear. And its name was Bruce—

"Mrs. Raymond?"

Karen turned quickly. A man was entering the office doorway from the hall. He nodded at her, moving up to the glass window of the reception desk. Reaching into his jacket, he pulled out a wallet and slid it across the counter as she approached.

"Sergeant Gordon."

She glanced at the I.D. Frank Gordon. LAPD, Homicide Division. She pushed the wallet back, managing a smile. "They said you'd be coming." In spite of herself, Karen felt a curious sense of relief now that he was here. She'd never thought the time would come when she would welcome the presence of a detective, but anything was better than being alone. "I suppose you want a statement?"

"That's right." Frank Gordon put his wallet away and glanced around the office. There was a sound of footsteps from the hall outside.

Karen felt the smile freeze on her face, but Gordon's nod was reassuring. "Don't be alarmed. We're going through the building. Was there anyone here when you came in?"

"No. At least I didn't see anybody."

"Don't worry, they'll check it out." Gordon glanced at Karen's purse on the counter top. "We can leave whenever you're ready."

"Where are we going?"

"My orders are to take you home and get your statement. After that—" Gordon shrugged.

"Did Lieutenant Barringer say anything about bringing me in to headquarters?"

"I'm to call him from your apartment." Gordon smiled ruefully. "Right now he's got other things on his mind."

Karen picked up her purse and stepped out into the reception area. Sergeant Gordon opened the hall door for her. The sound of footsteps grew louder, and as she moved past Gordon into the corridor, she saw the two uniformed officers converging from either side, holding service revolvers.

"Just a minute, lady," said the one on her left.

"It's okay." Gordon came up beside her and flashed his I.D. "I'm taking Mrs. Raymond home. Barringer's orders."

"Go ahead."

But the officers waited in the hall with them until the elevator arrived, and Karen noticed that neither of them holstered their weapons.

Two more patrolmen greeted them when the elevator door slid open on the lobby level, and once more Gordon identified himself. The lobby was otherwise deserted, and when they emerged onto the street, the traffic was moving in its regular rhythm. Aside from the squad cars parked along the curb, there was no reminder of what had happened.

Gordon led her around the corner. His car was parked on a lot down the block.

"What's your address?" he said, above the noise of the starting motor.

She was surprised he didn't know it, but gave it to him, adding, "Better not take the freeway. It's jammed at this hour."

Gordon glanced at the dashboard clock. "Shouldn't be, not at seven o'clock."

Karen frowned. "Is it that late already?"

He nodded. "Had anything to eat yet?"

"No."

"Maybe we could grab something on the way. I'll get your statement over dinner."

"I'm really not very hungry."

"Only a suggestion." But Karen could sense the disappointment in his voice. Probably starving, she told herself.

"I could use some coffee."

"Good enough." The car swung out onto the street. "Let's head out your way and find a place when we get off the freeway."

Gordon was silent during the drive; Karen wondered what he was thinking. About the statement, probably, and questions he was going to ask.

As for herself, she kept rehearsing the answers. Sergeant Gordon was one of the new breed of police officers, she decided: well-mannered, soft-spoken, obviously more intelligent than Forbes or poor Tom Doyle. But she remembered Sergeant Cole and Lieutenant Barringer, whose courtesy masked cold efficiency. She mustn't let politeness disarm her.

Karen studied Frank Gordon's profile as he drove. Brown hair, blue eyes, regular features. She wondered if he was married, and if so, what his wife thought about his spending the night alone with a strange woman.

Of course it was all in the line of duty. Guarding her, asking questions, trying to track down the murderer. If he succeeded, it'd probably mean a promotion and his wife would be proud.

But what would happen to Bruce?

CHAPTER 22

Up against the wall.

The phrase kept ringing in his head.

Up against the wall. Not to be confused with up the wall or around the bend. Stupid words, cruel words, joking and unfeeling references to the condition of a soul in torment.

What did they know, these stand-up comics who sniggered about flipping, blowing your mind, falling out of your tree? Nobody really understood, and there was only one way to find out. By sitting in an asylum cell night after night, listening to the screams—the screams that were coming from your own throat.

He'd learned to control the screams, of course; to control himself, and then to control others. The plan had worked, hadn't it? He'd sworn to get free and he was free.

But he was still up against the wall. All day long he'd had this feeling. Or had it been all day? Maybe it started when he saw Tom Doyle's face falling away, his arms flailing, his body spinning in empty air.

No, that had been necessary. Just as it had been necessary to spare Karen. Only for the time being, of course. Because she had to go, too. And she would go, soon. Sparing Karen had been part of the plan.

If he'd guessed right, it wouldn't be long now. If she did what he thought she would, went where he thought she'd go, then all the police in the world couldn't save her. And the body count would rise.

Until then, he was up against the wall.

But the wall was crumbling fast.

CHAPTER 23

The little restaurant was almost deserted, and Karen wondered about that. Business was usually so good here, particularly since the piano bar had begun operating.

Maybe people were afraid to come out at night, after what they'd read in the papers. And Tom Doyle's death would have been reported on the evening newscasts. Strange, in a way, to think of several million people being afraid of just one man. Maybe their fear sprang from the simple fact that they wouldn't be able to recognize him if they saw him.

And her fear was that she could.

Gordon was finishing dessert. He'd been mercifully casual in his questioning while they ate, but now, as he pushed his plate away and sat back, Karen knew the reprieve had ended.

He glanced at his watch. "I should be calling in soon," he said. "Maybe they've found your husband."

"Or the murderer," Karen said.

"You're a very loyal woman, aren't you, Mrs. Raymond?"

"Loyalty has nothing to do with it." Karen recognized the defensive note in her voice. "According to the law, a man is presumed innocent until he's proven guilty."

Frank Gordon sighed. "Let's lay it on the line, Mrs. Raymond. You're trying to protect one man because you believe—or say you believe—he might be innocent. What about all the others, the victims who died? We *know* they were innocent, but who protected them?"

Karen shook her head. "I still say Bruce had no motive. Why should he kill anyone to get out of the sanatorium when they were going to release him anyway?"

"Because he didn't know he was going to be released." Gordon watched her face as he spoke. "That's the truth, isn't it?"

You bastard, Karen thought. Lieutenant Barringer didn't guess, that police psychiatrist didn't find out, but *you* had to come up with it. *Yes, that's the truth.*

Gordon wasn't waiting for an answer. Maybe he didn't need an answer, maybe he read it in her face. "I can understand a wife's desire to save her husband. But you've got to understand our position, too. It's the job of the police to safeguard the citizens, and so far we've failed. Now we've got to think of the future. The man we suspect of those murders is still at large. And unless we can find him, quickly, we have every reason to believe others will die. Other innocent people."

"But my husband isn't the only one," Karen said. "There's another missing patient—Edmund Cromer."

"Who?" Gordon was sitting upright now. "Why didn't you give me that name before?"

"Because Bruce was going to tell Doyle." Karen's voice faltered. "Then, after what happened, I had no chance to—"

"Suppose you tell me now."

"Yes." And she did.

Gordon watched her, nodding from time to time as she repeated what Bruce had told her. His expression was noncommittal—the blank, official look—but he waited until she finished before he spoke.

"That's it?" he said.

"Yes. At least, that's all I can remember."

"No description?"

"He intended to give that information to Doyle—"

"So he said." Gordon's voice was flat.

"Don't you believe—"

"That your husband told you those things?" Gordon nodded. "The question is—why?"

"Because he wanted to identify the murderer."

"Or because he knew it was one way to lure Doyle to the roof and dispose of him. Then he could feel perfectly safe in coming after you."

"But he didn't—"

"Only because there was a second man on duty in the hall below, a man he hadn't known about. Seeing him must have scared your husband off."

"That still doesn't affect what he said about Cromer," Karen said.

"Let's think it over." Gordon spoke slowly. "Your husband implicated another patient in the murders. But did he offer anything tangible, anything that could be checked out as proof? What assurance is there he was telling you the truth? How can you even be sure that the other patient's name is Cromer?"

Karen didn't reply. Because, from somewhere inside, she heard the echo of Bruce's

234

voice answering for her. Standing up there on the roof with that grim smile, and saying, *Maybe there is no Edmund Cromer. Maybe I made the whole thing up.*

The inner echo faded. The room began to blur, and it was only the quick touch of Gordon's hand on hers that restored reality. "Mrs. Raymond—"

Reality. This hand, this voice. It was time to stop listening to lies, time to stop lying to herself. Karen blinked, opened her eyes wide.

"Better now?" Frank Gordon released her hand.

Karen nodded.

"One thing is certain. There is another patient. We'll have to check out the name now, try to find him. But you've got to prepare yourself for the possibility that he's totally innocent. And if so, it's highly probable that he's no longer alive."

Gordon spoke softly, but there was no denying the force of his logic. Denial was no longer possible.

"I've been thinking about what you told me earlier," he said. "And there's something that doesn't seem consistent."

"Consistent?"

"These killings are methodical, you know. Granted that the person responsible is considered clinically unbalanced, there's evidence of a high order of intelligence at work here. These are not the usual crimes of impulse or passion. We're faced with someone who is intent on killing anyone who can identify him. Which brings us to you."

"I don't understand."

"If your husband is responsible for what's happened, why would he consider you a threat to his safety? You've already identified him as an inmate of the sanatorium. Eliminating you now won't alter your testimony."

Karen took a deep breath. Maybe there was a reprieve, perhaps denial was still possible after all. "That's what I told them," she said. "Lieutenant Barringer and the others. He has no reason to harm me." Saying it again, she could half-believe it herself. "You're right, there's an inconsistency."

"A *seeming* inconsistency, I said." Gordon's voice was still soft, but she heard it all too clearly. "So there has to be another reason. Eliminating you won't alter your testimony. But it would prevent you from ever being able to alter it yourself."

His eyes were level with hers, and there was no reprieve in them after all. "Mrs. Raymond—why did your husband commit himself to the sanatorium?"

No reprieve, no denial. Too many had died,

and who could say where it would stop unless she stopped it?

"We had a quarrel." The words came quickly now, it was like vomiting up something ugly, something which had to come out. "I told him he hadn't been acting like himself, not since he came back, and that he needed help. I told him I wanted him to see a doctor."

"What was his response?"

"He said he'd think it over. And then he quieted down. Did I want to go for a drive, he asked. So we did, and neither of us talked about it anymore. It was as though bringing it out in the open had somehow relieved us both, and I remembered thinking maybe I'd been making a mountain out of a molehill, he was just nervous and upset about not working. We went to Wright's, the way we used to do before we were married. And when we came home, we made love."

Karen lowered her glance, but the words kept coming. "I fell asleep then. And when I woke up, I was choking, I couldn't breathe. Because he was on top of me again, his hands around my neck—squeezing and squeezing—

"Somehow I managed to fight him off. I hit him in the face and he fell back. That's when his eyes opened. All this time they'd been closed, and later he said he'd been asleep, it was a nightmare, he didn't know what he was doing. He seemed to be in a state of shock.

"The next day he called Dr. Griswold."

"He tried to kill you." Gordon's eyes never left her face. "And you're the only one who knows?"

"Yes. Except for Rita."

"Rita?"

"His sister. She'd never tell—"

"Where is she now?"

Karen told him. "But she's already talked to the police. They even searched to make sure he wasn't hiding out there."

"Does she have any protection now?"

"A bodyguard? I don't think so. But even if Bruce came there, she'd be safe. She loves her brother, she wouldn't betray him."

"Can Bruce be sure of that?"

Karen hesitated.

Gordon rose. "We're going out there right now," he said. "And then I'm taking both of you downtown. You two should have been held in security from the beginning. And you would have been, if you'd told us the truth."

"But I swear she's not in danger—"

"Swear?" Gordon shook his head. "All you can do now is pray. And even that may be too late."

CHAPTER 24

That night the searchlights swept the sky.

Their brilliance flooded the Music Center, where the Beautiful People preened for cameras recording their presence at yet another gala charity benefit. Other people, less beautiful and entirely uncapitalized, saw the distant radiance from the windows of hospital wards where they lay dying or giving birth or whatever they do in dreary places that are never pictured in the society section.

Light lanced upward from the Grand Opening of a supermarket, danced down from aerial beacons on the far hills, hovered from police helicopters crisscrossing the city.

But there were dark places too. Cemeteries for the resting dead. Side streets for the living who could not rest because of what they'd read in the papers, heard on the news, pictured in their own minds, as they huddled behind locked doors.

Bolts and bars were no protection against the invasion of fear. The favored few were able to pretend nothing had happened. But for the many there were only shadows in which strange shapes stirred.

The airport was neither light nor dark. A gray mist crept in from the west, blurring the beacons, shrouding the shadows with silver.

Karen remembered the fog she'd driven through on that other evening. It was forty-eight hours ago, yet it seemed a lifetime away. And for some, it was literally just that. A lifetime vanished forever, swallowed up in gray oblivion.

But there were lights here, too, like the one streaming from the office window of Raymond's Charter Service. And there were shadows off to the blind side of the frame structure where Frank Gordon pulled up and parked his car.

Karen started to open the door on the passenger side, but Gordon's hand moved to her arm in quick restraint.

"Wait."

He peered through the windshield, scanning the airstrip, the runways, the dark cluster of hangars bordering the field behind and beyond the office. Nothing moved in the mist.

"Now."

Karen slid out of her seat and crossed behind the car as Gordon emerged. He was holding a service revolver.

"Keep behind me," he said. "Behind, and to one side."

He started towards the office, moving close to the wall, away from the fan of light coming from the window. The window was on the far side of the door, so they approached in shadow: shadow, and clammy mist.

The door was slightly ajar. As Gordon reached it, he gestured for Karen to halt.

"Back," he murmured. The revolver rose in readiness.

He kicked the door open.

Then he stood there. Stood there for a moment, or an eternity. Time stopped for Karen; everything stopped until he turned, and spoke.

"Nothing. Nobody here."

She joined him then, moved with him into the lighted office. The floor fan droned, its turbulence fluttering the papers pinned to the wall.

Gordon glanced at the desk top. Rita's purse rested there, next to the telephone. Beside it, in the big ashtray, a crushed cigarette butt still smoldered. Karen noted it and nodded.

"She must have just stepped out."

Gordon frowned. "What makes you so sure? I didn't see any car when we drove up."

"Rita drives a VW. She generally parks it inside the hangar."

"The one in back?"

"Yes—in back and to the right."

He nodded and turned. Karen followed him through the doorway. At the right of the clapboard shack was a tied-down plane, a single-engine Cessna. Gordon halted in its shadow, staring at the dark opening of the hangar beyond. Somewhere off inside, a faint light flickered.

Karen started to step forward, but Frank Gordon shook his head.

"Not yet."

Peering into the hangar, Karen could make out the squat bulk of the VW. Behind it was a plane, and beyond that, the light. Its source was apparently an electric lantern, placed on the floor beside a tool rack. And now Rita's silhouette moved across it.

"That her?" Gordon's voice was pitched to a whisper.

"Yes, thank God. And she's alone."

"Good. Here's what I want you to do. Go in and talk to her."

"You're not coming with me?"

Gordon gestured with the revolver. "Don't worry—if you need me, I'll be ready. My hunch is you'll get further with her if she doesn't see me at first. Tell her what happened—about Bruce, and Tom Doyle. I think she's ready to crack. Maybe Bruce has been in touch with her, maybe she knows where he is."

"What if she won't say anything?"

"Then I'll take over. But it's worth a chance." Gordon put his hand on her arm. "Remember, she's in danger, too, whether she knows it or not. You've got to convince her of that."

"I'll try."

Karen moved through the mist, moved forward to the deeper darkness beyond the hangar entrance.

And now there was no turning back.

No turning back as she walked past the plane, no turning back as she emerged into the fitful flicker of the light, no turning back as Rita looked up and saw her, recognized her.

"What are you doing here?"

There was shrill surprise in the voice, and

something else, something more than mere surprise, in the shadowed face.

"I have to talk to you. Now."

Rita had a heavy wrench in her hand. She didn't put it down; instead, her fingers tightened around the handle.

"You picked a fine time. Can't you see I'm busy?"

"I didn't pick the time. Please, Rita, listen to me—"

"I'm listening."

She listened while Karen told her about Bruce's call, the meeting on the roof and what followed. From time to time Karen hesitated, but she didn't stop completely until she came to the moment when she'd stared out of the window at the body sprawled far below.

Rita didn't move, her face was still in shadow, and she said absolutely nothing.

I'm not reaching her, Karen told herself. *I have no way of reaching her, only words.*

She found them.

"You didn't see what I saw, Rita. Tom Doyle, lying in the street with his head smashed open like a rotten melon. Griswold dead in a room filled with the smell of his own burning flesh. That poor nurse—"

"What do you want from me?"

"The truth." Karen felt her fingers curl back against the palms, felt the nails, digging into flesh. "It's not a matter of faith or loyalty—it can't be, not anymore. We've got to stop what's happening. If you've kept anything back, if you know where Bruce has been hiding—"

"She didn't know."

It was Bruce's voice.

And it was Bruce who now stepped from the shadows on the far side of the plane.

Karen stared at him as he came towards her, nodding slowly.

"I headed here the other night," he said. "But Rita didn't know it. I didn't want to involve her, any more than I did you. But I needed some place where I'd be safe, and this was all I could think of. When the police arrived to question her, I managed to stow myself away in a plane on the field and they didn't find me. After they were gone, I left. It wasn't until this evening, when I came back, that I let her know I was here, told her what had happened."

"Then she knows—you confessed—"

"There is nothing to confess."

"But I saw you on the roof! I sent Doyle to you myself!"

"He didn't find me." Bruce's voice was low. "After you left to get him, I lost my nerve. I couldn't face him—I was afraid—so I ran. Karen, believe me, I swear to God I was out of the building before he ever reached that roof!"

"Then who killed him?"

"Cromer."

It wasn't a statement. It was a shocked murmur of recognition, as Bruce stared past Karen—stared at the man who now entered the hangar, holding the revolver in his hand.

Karen saw him, and then she turned to Bruce and there was no stopping now. "You're crazy!" she gasped. "This is Sergeant Gordon—he's a detective—"

The man smiled. "Nobody's crazy," he said softly. "Not your husband. And certainly not me." The smile was as fixed and steady as the weapon he held in his hand.

"I was waiting outside the office building today, hoping your husband would try to contact you. When he went to the roof, I followed him. It seemed like a perfect opportunity to dispose of the only remaining person who could identify me. I'd managed to find all the others, and now, through the exercise of logic, I've found Bruce."

He nodded, eyes on Karen. "Logic, I said. Cold, clear logic. But your arrival prevented me from carrying out my intentions. I stayed concealed on the far side of the skylight and listened. When Bruce revealed my name, I realized the plan must change. Because there were now two people who knew my name.

And I couldn't deal with you both there, not without a weapon."

"So you let her go, and when I ran off, you waited for Doyle," Bruce said.

"Exactly. I was behind him when he came up through the skylight exit, and he never knew what happened."

Karen shuddered. "And Frank Gordon?"

"I was waiting in a service closet down the hall outside your office when he arrived. I found a heavy metal doorstop among the storage articles. It's not there now, but Gordon is, unless they've discovered him by now. I took his gun and his badge and I.D. The car, of course, is one I'd picked up earlier today."

"I was alone when you came to me in the office," Karen said. "You had the revolver—"

"Logic." The man smiled again. "It would have been dangerous to do anything with the police right outside the door, searching the building. The important thing was to get you out of there. And I was still hoping you could lead me to Bruce again. When you told me what you did at dinner, I knew that Rita was also a problem. So let's have no more of this stupid name-calling. My thinking was correct. You're here, all of you." The smile was still fixed, but his finger tightened on the trigger.

"Cromer, listen to me." Bruce faced the smile, faced the muzzle of the gun. "I talked it over with Rita before you came, told her everything. She said I should call the police—and I did, from her office. They'll be arriving any moment now—"

Cromer's voice was as cold as his smile. "Please, don't insult my intelligence. That's the oldest gag in the world—"

Then the cold smile froze.

Because he heard the sirens, sounding in the distance.

They all heard them, but it was Rita who moved.

Her arm came up, holding the wrench. And then she hurled it at Cromer's head.

He flung himself against the side of the plane as the wrench whizzed by, thudded to the floor beyond. The revolver came up and he fired.

On the heels of the shattering echo, Karen heard Rita cry out. She fell back, clutching her arm. Amidst a swirl of acrid smoke, Karen saw the blood spurting from between Rita's fingers, saw Bruce lunge forward to grapple with Cromer.

Cromer gripped the gun, fighting to turn the barrel of the weapon towards Bruce's chest. But Bruce chopped at his wrist and the revolver fell.

For an instant the smoke parted and Karen saw Cromer clearly. The smile was gone, the semblance of humanity itself seemed stripped away, and all that remained was the animal fury of glaring eyes and snarling mouth—the naked face of violence.

Then Cromer's clubbed fists smashed against Bruce's chest, hurling him back. He turned and ran out of the hangar, into the mist of the night.

The sirens shrieked from the roadway, and Cromer swerved. Through the open end of the hangar, Karen could see him running across the field.

A dark blur descended from the sky, then exploded in a sudden blaze of revolving light. Karen screamed then, but her voice was lost in the roar of the helicopter blades spinning down on the fleeing figure. By the time the pilot saw Cromer through the shrouding fog, it was too late to avoid him.

The helicopter dipped, almost toppled, as the shearing metal struck. Cromer fell and his body ceased to move.

But his head rolled halfway down the field.

CHAPTER 25

There were two ambulances—one for Rita, one for what was left of Cromer.

Lieutenant Barringer arrived and took over.

Bruce made his statement and Karen made hers. Even Rita was able to give a preliminary deposition while the police surgeon applied the tourniquet to her arm.

Then it was time to make the trip down to the Van Nuys Station, time to make the tapes and sign the transcripts. For a while it seemed as though it would never end, but eventually, of course, it did.

Free, Karen told herself. *Finally free*.

And she and Bruce walked out.

Into the night-world . . .

THE BEST IN HORROR

JOHN FARRIS

"America's premier novelist of terror. When he turns it on, nobody does it better." —Stephen King

"Farris is a giant of contemporary horror!"

—Peter Straub

Ramsey Campbell

☐ 51652-4	DARK COMPANIONS		$3.50
51653-2		Canada	$3.95
☐ 51654-0	THE DOLL WHO ATE HIS		$3.50
51655-9	MOTHER	Canada	$3.95
☐ 51658-3	THE FACE THAT MUST DIE		$3.95
51659-1		Canada	$4.95
☐ 51650-8	INCARNATE		$3.95
51651-6		Canada	$4.50
☐ 58125-3	THE NAMELESS		$3.50
58126-1		Canada	$3.95
☐ 51656-7	OBSESSION		$3.95
51657-5		Canada	$4.95

Buy them at your local bookstore or use this handy coupon:
Clip and mail this page with your order

TOR BOOKS—Reader Service Dept.
49 W. 24 Street, 9th Floor, New York, NY 10010

Please send me the book(s) I have checked above. I am enclosing
$_____ (please add $1.00 to cover postage and handling).
Send check or money order only—no cash or C.O.D.'s.

Mr./Mrs./Miss _____
Address _____
City _____ State/Zip _____
Please allow six weeks for delivery. Prices subject to change
without notice.

GRAHAM MASTERTON